Office Drama...The Story Will Never End

Clarita Vaughn

Dedicated to my Father God in Heaven; my husband and to my

family, who have encouraged me to stand strong on: "I can do all things through Christ who strengthens me."

Philippians 4:13

Chapter 1

Digital

If you were ever part of the working class at one time or another, you have witnessed or even been involved in some type of issue at the job. It could be the gossip out of the break room or what's really going on behind closed doors. About 80 percent of the time, the things I hear about are hilarious; and I can't wait to get home and spread the news to my honey. I think I'm getting way ahead of myself. Not wanting you to think I'm perfect in any fashion, no sir. I just like to listen.

Going home to my honey, Digital, is always the best part of my day. We have been married for about 12 years now. We're a typical family, with two kids, a big house, cool family and nice friends. I met Digital when I was just 20 years old. I was fresh in a new town and out of a bad relationship; he was a true gentleman. My parents just moved to Fresno, California for work, and I was hot on their tails. Running away from a man is not an issue. Running away from a man when you just had his baby, his wife is out to get you and he is on drugs, is nothing to mess with. I figured, get my life back on track and then worry about baby daddy drama later.

Digital worked in the oil and gas industry as a contract administrator. I was also in that line of work, so I reached out to friends I knew would help me to get a job. In the beginning I worked and went straight home. My parents were not very happy with me and the last man in my life. The best thing I could do was walk on eggshells for awhile. I only saw Digital in passing before we even has a serious conversations. That first conversation came with a funny ending.

"So, new girl, how do you say your name again?" he said. God, I get tired of people asking me that. Why couldn't my mom name me something simply, like Lucy or Tina? "It's Chani, like Shaunie O'Neal, just spelled differently!" He smiled. "I liked how you used the sports reference. It's the best way to get my attention."

"Oh really, and why is that?" I asked.

"Man, I'm a sport genius. I know any and everything about most sports. I keep trying to tell everyone, I'm the best in the business, but they never believe me."

Side note and pointer for any guy who needs help in the babe department: if you are trying to get a lady's attention, laughter is the best medicine. Talking to Digital, I was popping pills. I could not stop smiling.

Trust me, I was trying to. Digital was that smooth dark chocolate brother that you just want to sink your teeth into. Dark wavy short hair that was always neatly cut. It went very well with his goatee, which outlines his lips. Not too thin and not to thick. Very kissable. His strong but silent build made you want to get to know him more. Nothing on him jiggled, all muscle.

I'm pretty tall for a woman at 5 feet, 10 inches, and he towered over me. That is all I could get from a quick overview and man I wanted to know more about him. In this company you had the folks who worked in the office, like Digital and me, and then you had the people who worked out in the field. The common ground for all of us was the company breakroom. Working in the business office, we had to always be professional. Digital knew how to make the suits work for him. I always wondered where he purchased his clothing; they seemed tailored made to fit perfectly on his body. Another trait about Digital that I would truly grow to appreciate is his very straightforward personality. You can speak to him and expect nothing but the truth, no sugar-coating. Even with that type of personality, he was very smart and humble.

"So how do you get folks to know that you are the best?" He looked at me with confidence and said, "All I do is win." That was it, as corny as it was, I burst out laughing. He was smiling because he knew he had me.

After 12 years of ups and downs, we find ourselves back in my hometown of Austin, Texas. Digital knew that I always wanted to move back home and we figured it was a good move for our family. The cost of living was way cheaper and the school system was designed to focus on our children's educational needs. The department he worked in allowed for him to transfer his position to Texas. I was not so lucky. It took me about a month, but I was able to find a job with a sister company. I had to start my career over, but I'm determined to move up that corporate ladder like I did in California.

One thing about marriage that always helps is communicating with each other. I was the one who had to find a way to break the silence. I did not like to talk much. I found other ways to express myself. Digital, on the other hand, knew how to express himself very well. When he was upset, he would never stop talking. I would keep still hoping he would just shut up. So that we could come together on a happier note, we developed a special time in our lives that made us laugh and brought us closer together. At times there were learning lessons involved that made us say, "We know what not to do." A lot of folks, men especially, think that sex will always keep a marriage strong or at least their side of it. Trust me, it helps, oh yes and when it is *THE BOMB*, it truly helps. Our special time comes with a little twist. We call it *Office Drama* time. We come together each week with a story or something that has happened on the job. Not trying to top each other, just bringing joy, conversation and fun to our lives.

Chapter 2

Doctor, Doctor

As always I was home before Digital. I arrive at the office early so that I'm home before the bus drops our kid's home. Knowing it was Office Drama night, I hurried through the house, making sure everything was in order for us to chill. Dinner is ready, the kids' homework is complete. I made sure my boo has a nice bath ready so we could start our night off right. "Blake, Isis, dad's home." I could hear the garage door open as they ran downstairs. "Hi daddy," is their standard greeting. Little Isis always jumping on her dad's back trying to pretend she is stronger than he is. Blake is a teenager so he plays it cool these days. Instead, he'll give his dad a high-five as he walks through the house.

"OK, monsters, off to your rooms. Kitchen closes at 8:30 p.m. if you want anything else." Time restrictions have to be put in place so that my kids don't eat us out of house and home. As the kids go back upstairs, I grab Digital by the waist and squeeze him tightly. He gives me an extra squeeze, sucking the air from me. I try to kiss his soft lips and as always he turns his head. I get a nice kiss of a new beard forming. "Thanks, I like to the taste of hard work in the afternoon. How was your day?"

"It was work, just happy that it is over. What's for dinner?"

"Lemon-pepper grilled chicken with mac and cheese and boiled corn." As he unloads his works pockets, he smiles and asks if I was ready for the Office Drama story of the night. "Something is wrong with the people I work with, if they think they can get away with some stuff."

"Wait, wait, don't tell me yet. I want to eat and get relaxed." He smiles and said, "OK, let's get it started."

After eating dinner and listening to the kids talk about their day, we start preparing the house for the night. The kids have had their showers and items for the next day of school were put in their proper place, so that we were not scrambling in the morning.

"Love you guys, good night and say your prayers."

Turing off all the lights, Digital chases me through the dark to our room. He is a very touchy feely person and knows how to use his hands well. He grabbed me from behind and pulled me close to him.

As much as I did not want him to stop, I had to remind him that it is our night to conversate. He takes a deep breath and lets me go. After taking a nice hot bath together, we climb into bed with anticipation of the story of the night.

One thing about Digital that I mentioned early on is that he is corny. That side has never changed. After laughing continually for about five minutes, Digital takes a deep breath and called his story "Fake Doctor's Note." After wiping the tears from his eyes, he begins to replay his story for me in great detail. "OK, working in an office with a bunch of fools can always be interesting. At any time there are at least 30 people in the company break room. Today, an employee was taken out the break room by our bosses without any questions. After some digging by the cubical snitch

Levi and putting some of the past events in place, we finally understood what happened.

"When it comes to calling in sick, there are a few ways you can work it with the company, depending on your standings. The company allows you so many call-ins before you are walked out the door. If you go past 10 points, you are out. In our contract, if you bring in a doctor's note, you will not lose a point.

"About six months ago, Gavin, who has been with the company for about five years and work the construction pipeline crew in the yard, started to call into work on the day he was suppose to return from his two days off. He was doing this about twice a month. Gavin would bring in his doctor's note in an envelope labeled with a local doctor, who some of the other guys use as well from time to time. We didn't think anything of it at first, but it started to get so often and obvious we had to ask."

I chuckled and said "and men think chicks are nosey."

Digital rolled his eyes and smiled. "Anyway, back to my story, we had to ask him what's up? Is everything OK?" Gavin, in a deep Southern slurred voice said, 'Yeah man. It's good and all that.' Just his expression, like a kid in a candy store, made us wonder what was really going on. Logan, another co-worker, asked, 'Give us some details man? Why all the call-ins?' Gavin stood by his 'I was sick' story for awhile. I noticed he was waiting until there were only a few people left in the breakroom before he would say anything else," Digital said.

"After about 30 minutes of Logan and some of the other guys nagging him, he finally starts to let us know the deal. 'Man, there was this bad-ass chick down at the gas station. Not sure what she is, Mexican, Philippine, hell I don't know and I don't care, but she has ass like Nikki, Nikki, Nikki. Her legs went on for miles and miles. She's all muscle with a nice tan. Not too light, not too dark, just right. Her breast was like two soft king-sized pillows. The face was OK, but that is something anyone can deal with.'" Now mind you, as Gavin is letting us in on his after-work activities, thinking back to previous conversations with him, a strong point came to mind. This darn dude is married.

"Logan asked, 'Man, what you did with all of that?' He replied, 'After checking her out, she came up to me and commented on my looks. She was jocking the work uniform. She told me 'I like a man who works hard and looks good doing it.' Everyone in the break-room had to stop and laugh. From that line when knew she was playing him. From my point of view, Gavin is an ugly man. He is only about 5 feet tall, but weighs at least 250 to 275 pounds. Our company has a great dental plan, but this dude never took advantage of it. His teeth are all jacked up, but when a bad-ass chick like that is giving you some attention, all you can do it take it. He melted right into her hands and she knew how to work her magic on him.

"'Her name was Morgana and she had my nose wide open. It started slow. Juicy, the nickname she said she liked to be called, knew there was a shorty at home. She did not care. She just wanted me to hook her up with Big Willy. On my sick days, saying that with a ton of sarcasm, it was all about Juicy. Took her to the movies, shopping and out to lunch. At night we hit the clubs and I tore that ass up. It was all about her, whatever she wanted. After a few weeks, she told me she was having some issues and need help with her rent. Had to move some funds around, but taking care and keeping her happy was all there was at this time.'"

Wait, wait, I had to interrupt. "You mean to tell me that this chick has this man going crazy like that? That he would put her before his own family. I don't get it." Digital smiled and said "men that let the monkey control them do some stuff that you would never believe. Some men lust after it and cannot see past it, until it is too late."

Gavin told us that she can do some things in the bedroom that would just freak you out. It was like nothing that he was getting at home.

I asked, "Did he ever ask?" Digital chuckled and said "probably not." By this time, he had all our attention. Logan asks for some extra detail about their bedroom fun. He said she has a stripper pole in her bedroom. She teases him with dances. She climbs the pole, spins around and slides down with her legs all the way opened. She is really good at making the booty cheeks bounce. Juicy knew how to work her lips and her mouth.

"According to Gavin, there were times when they did not even have sex. He was just so tired from all the foreplay. She was very adventurous and was not afraid to get her man off anywhere."

"Now that's a woman with some skills," I said with a curious look on my face. "You need to get with Gavin and get her number; I need to learn some stuff."

Digital looked at me with a look of *for real* in his eyes. He had to blink a few times to get that image of me on a pole out of his head. I laughed and told him to finish his story before he was also too tired without even having sex.

"So it has been six months and now he found out that Juicy is going to have his baby. The breakroom went silent. Levi shouted out, 'Man, you fucking that girl without a rubber?' We all shook our heads. DUMBASS is all that was on my mind. While we all were in deep thought, the supervisor walked in and asked Gavin to come to his office. At first we did not think much of it. Levi got up from the table where were sitting at to get a soda out of the machine when he notices Gavin being walked out the door by the supervisor. He took a step back and made a sound to get our attention. We all looked at him at once and he said. 'I think Gavin just lost his job.'"

"He told us what he just saw, so one by one, we funneled out the break room back to our desks. Sure enough, the other supervisors on the floor were cleaning out his locker. The only thing that was on my mind was that this dumbass has a wife and kids at home, plus a chick he's messing with is pregnant. I got back to work because it wasn't clear as to why he was fired and I did not want to get mixed up in that situation. About an hour goes by and Levi comes over to my desk and asks me to help him get something out his car. I looked at him with a raised eyebrow, and say, 'What's wrong with you?' Levi had this look of determination on his face. Eyes wide open, he asks again. Taking a deep breath and looking at him, I got up and took the trip to the parking look. Man, it was hot outside so I thought whatever was on Levi's mind better be good.

"After we get to his car, Levi opened his truck and pretended to search for some invisible object. 'Digital, do you want to know why Galvin was fired?' Levi is a very hyper individual. He has this high-pitched East Coast voice. When he speaks he is so loud you can hear him over anyone. 'Hell yeah, why did they walk him up out of here?' Levi started to laugh, which made me laugh. Hell, I don't know why I was laughing, but he was cracking up."

Digital could not help himself, but he started to laugh again. I just looked at him with this blank look on my face. "Boy, finish the story." After laughing for another five minutes he said Levi pulled out some papers from his back pocket.

"This fool had gone into the supervisor's office after they went to lunch to see what the deal was with Gavin. He saw the termination papers on the supervisor's desk and saw the reason for termination was due to falsified documents. Right under it was one of Gavin's doctor's notes. Levi handed it to me to read and when I tell you, I laughed until I could not breathe, man, I laughed to the point my chest hurt."

Again, Digital started to laugh. "Tell me, tell me what the note said." I was on pens and needles.

Digital finally calmed down and read the note as best as he could recall:

Patient: GAVIN MOORE

Date: July 12, 2012

To Whom It May Concern:

This is to confirm I have seen and evaluated the above-named patient. This patient WUZ sick on the dates listed below and should be excused from work.

"Oh my God, are you telling me this man lost his job because his dumbass could not spell. Are you serious?" I asked.

Digital was on the floor laughing and I was right there with him. Some people are so stupid. Digital, now that was a story. Still chuckling and with tears in our eyes we climb back into bed, lights out.

Chapter 3

Love and Marriage

Life is so good for my family and me. We are truly blessed and thank God each day for the blessing. It may sound mean that we chat about other people's lives or what we see on the job, but we feel that it is our time. The kids are growing so fast. Before we know it, it will only be Digital and I. If we don't know how to enjoy each other now, we will go crazy once the kids are gone. It did take us time to get to this point.

Digital is as tough as they come. He is a true leader. Surrounded by drugs and gangs, he never let that remove him from focus or goals. Sports are his outlet. Anything his parents could get him in, he excelled at it. The only thing that held him back from moving to a professional level in sports was his asthma.

It would sideline him at times. He was still able to go to a local college using a sports scholarship, but knowing that he would never play professional, he went after his Master's Degree in business. When I first met him, I knew that brother was smart, but learning more about his career path just wowed me. The company he works for recruited him right after college and he has been on the upward path ever since. Meeting me was a big shock for not only him, but his family as well. In the beginning of our relationship, his family did not like that fact that I had a kid and some drama that could potentially follow. No matter how nice I was, they looked at me as handicapped.

When Digital and I had our first conversation, I was very nervous and my confidence level was super low. He was a great cheerleader. Never once did he let me hang my head down. He was always complimenting on how good I looked. I have to say, I was pretty sexy for someone who just had a baby. I had the height and I was all legs. I was not built like the typical Southern girl. I was very skinny, just barley meeting the 110-pound mark on the scale. I had enough booty to palm like a basketball and average-size breast. Thank God for *Vicki Don't Tell No Body*. Gives a girl all the cleavage she could hope for. My skin is as smooth caramel and long dark hair flowing down my back. If I did not have it straight down my back, it was up in a ponytail. In the beginning I did not smile much because my two front teeth were uneven. Girls, stop sucking your thumbs! One of my best features are my eyes. They are true window to my soul and my emotions. My eyes cannot hide anything. Anger, happiness, even worry, it would always show in my eyes. Digital was a key factor in getting me back on pace with who I truly was. I found myself lost after all the drama with my son's father. Digital pushed me to go back to school and worked on things that matter to me. My look was a key factor and getting my teeth fixed was one of the goals on my list. I knew this man truly loved me, but I would find a way to hurt him nonetheless.

After his family saw that even with a child that was not his, Digital was standing by my side; they backed off and accepted me into the family. That does not mean it was always laughter and fun times, but we all found a way to come together. Digital made it clear to not only me, but to his family as well, "This is who I want to be with so deal with it." He's always straight to the point. After dating for two years we were married in the church he grew up in and I joined to be by his side. My family did not like that because I grew up Catholic and changing my religion to a non-denominational church was frowned upon. After several attempts to change my mind, they backed off as well. Hey, I was going to church after not even caring about it for 10 years.

One thing about marriage and time, you are able to teach each other some tricks and you are able to open up to who you are really like. Digital is a very sexual person. When we were first married he would tell me he could not sleep until he was able to "bust a nut" in his words.   We played like newlyweds for a long time. After a few years of just sex he asked, "How come you don't like sex as much as I do?" That was a great question that I really never thought about, so I gave it some deep thought and explained to him, "It is not the fact that I don't like sex, but sex in our marriage is one-sided. It really is about what you like and making sure you get off. I do it to make you happy, but after that I'm just stuck."

"How can I make you happy? What can I do to make sure we both enjoy each other and that it is not one-sided?" Another great set of questions that I had to think about. Ladies, we get so wrapped up in our marriages that we tend to forget what we liked, love and cherished. You start to build your world around your spouse. That is why I truly believe some people cannot survive on their own because they forget who they are. So with that, I gave him a few starter pointers that we would build on and that would help us come closer together:

1. Be gentle. Don't grab me like you are gripping a golf club. Treat me like a baby.

Something so precious, you would be heartbroken if you break it.

2. Take your time. For me, it takes me a little while to get to that point of ecstasy. Get me there. Once I'm there every touch will be like fire.

3. Use your fingertips to caress my skin. The smallest touch turns me on the most. It means you are paying attention to my reaction and my body.

4. Relax your tongue just like using your fingertips. Smooth strokes.

5. Find my spots and kiss them, take care of them.

"Just starting off with these tips will help us come closer together. You will learn so much about me and about my body, and all you will ever want to do is learn more."

Chapter 4

Ayden and Brooke

With me being out of work for a month, I did not have any stories to bring to the table. So I was so excited to finally have a story to share with my boo.

"Digital, I have a story to share with you tonight."

"Well, it is about time, you have to pull your weight around here, too much on my shoulders. It is stressing me out."

"You are such a clown, hurry up I'm ready," I said.

"What! You are ready. Girl, I'm ready, too. I'm always ready."

I laughed, "You are so nasty. I mean, I'm ready to tell my story."

"OH, my bad. I thought you were ready for big daddy."

Lawd, the things I have to put up with. He smiled and asked what my story is about. All I could say was that love is on the air.

Even though I work for Digital's sister company, our office is set up a little different. We handle more of the financial and HR side of the company. This is strictly a business office. There are more ladies on the floor than men, so a whole lot of drama is always going down.

"When we do have men in the office, the chicks act like desperate housewives. The more dominate women try to claim stake to the guys. These girls would show them different levels of attention. This story caught my attention because the couple married after working at the office for a year. Brooke and Johnny was a cute couple. They were always at each other's desk when they could spare some time and, of course, lunch was together."

Digital, upon hearing this, said. "As much as I love you, I need time a part. That is just too much."

I agree with him and often wondered that myself. I just figured some people like to stay up under each other all the time. Brooke was a cute girl. She was a true redhead with the pale white skin to go with it. She hated the summers because she complained about her skin burning so fast. Her body was portioned just right with long legs and a nice chest. She was missing the famous booty, but white chicks don't get that special feature too often. She was a charmer to the ones that she knew she had to have on her side. To anyone she did not care for, you knew it.   Brooke and I had a working relationship. We worked really well with each other because we both had a strong drive and determination to move up in the company. Her husband Johnny was a nice-looking brother. They were the same height, but he was very skinny. He wore glasses and kept his hair fixed up in dreadlocks. I always wanted to ask him if he played basketball at one time or another, but I try to keep personal conversations down to a minimal.

"THAT'S RIGHT," Digital stated in his more demanding voices. "Keep it business only."

"Is that jealousy I detect?" I was smiling ear-to-ear awaiting his answer and he just turned his head away from me. Digital was very jealous, but I brought that mess on this marriage.

"Sorry, I did not mean to pick at you. Just finish the story!"

I could tell that our night could take a turn for the worse if I don't get back to the goods. "OK, like I said, Brooke and Johnny had been married for a year. I'm not sure how long they dated. Brooke has kids from a previous relationship, but none with Johnny. About a month ago a man by the name of Ayden transfers to our office from the Chicago area. Ayden worked in the yard at one time and worked his way up the professional ladder. We had the spot open for a floor supervisor and it was given to him."

"Wasn't that the job you applied for?"

"Yes, but they said I did not have enough experience."

"Hell, how do they expect you to get any if they don't give you a chance? You are a true leader and you step up when they need you to. I told you stop doing the extra stuff. They are just taking advantage of you."

"I know boo, but that is corporate America. You have to know someone to get into those types of jobs," I replied, getting back to my story.

"Ayden knew another supervisor on the floor, so that opened up doors for him. Ayden is a basic brother. He is an older gentleman, well maybe 10 years older than us. He has a medium build with a salt-and-pepper low top going. He reminded me of a high school coach from the 1970's. After having a few meetings with him, I can tell that he has a lot to learn on this job. One thing he does know how to do is play. He is a true playboy. And before you ask, yes he has a wife at home with kids."

"Why do you call him a playboy or think he is?"

"Well, you know I notice a lot of things and don't brush them off as most people do. The first thing I notice and mind you, this is only after seeing him in action for a week, are his hands. He loves to touch you when he talks. He got the hint really fast when I jerked my shoulder away on his attempt to be friendly. One person that has taken a liking to him is Brooke. It started with him stopping by and chatting about the ends and outs of the office. He hands always at the small of her back or on her shoulder. She would fling her shiny red hair to the side and give him a bright smile. Fanning him with her eyelashes and making him melt with her big green eyes.

"I think one of the ladies on the floor caught me sticking my finger in my mouth as if I was making myself throw up after I saw them flirting, and hearing Brooke's famous flirtatious laugh. We both had to laugh at my immaturity. Someone else who noticed those little flares was Johnny. He was a cool cat about it at first. He pulled Ayden off to the side and let him know that was not a territory that he should mark. Ayden explained to him that it was innocent, but we all knew better and we all knew Brooke. She saw an opportunity.

"Right away you could see and feel the change with the happy couple. Brooke would work through lunch and Johnny would be in the break room alone. One day I notice Brooke was in the office and Johnny wasn't. I asked her if he was OK, and she rolled her eyes saying that dead beat did not want to get out of bed. He said he was sick. I just told her that I would pray for him and walked off. She smacked her lips and said whatever. About an hour after that, Ayden came by and asked Brooke to come to his office. As they walked away, you could see all the heads popping up through cubical lane."

"What was that it you said, men are messy, I think both men and women are dead even," Digital said.

I laughed and said, "I will have to agree because I was looking, too. As the door closed behind them, one can only image what was going on. Brooke came out about 30 minutes later, tears running down her face. I was concerned so I went over to her desk and asked if she was OK. She shook her head and she explained how sad and depressed she was. I asked her to take a break so that we could chat. We went into the break room and she told me how it was hell at home. Johnny was always yelling and screaming. He even would slap her around from time to time.

"As she was telling me this, I figured this was the same story she was giving Ayden. She found a way in and will milk that cow until it is dry. I jumped on that bandwagon also just to see how far it would go. 'Brooke, I'm so sorry that you are going through that at home. I cannot image going through that. I pulled some tissue out my purse and handed it to her.'"

"Chani, you are so sweet. There is a lot about me you don't know. Growing up it was so hard and I had it harder by always having the wrong guy in my life."

I gave her a small hug and said "it will be OK." I then asked "would she be OK going home. I was truly worried about her. No matter what the drama is, no one should be abused." The tears dried up instantly and she said, 'Girl, I'm not worried about that shit I have at home anymore. I'm leaving his stupid ass.' I guess the look on my face was shocking because she laughed. 'What, did you think I was really going to stay with someone like that? Girl please, Ayden said he would help me find a place. We are leaving work early to go shop around.' "

"Now that is a woman on a mission," Digital said with a smile on his face.

"I know, right. I did not expect her to put up with it, but dang she does not waste any time. The next day Brooke was in the office and she was smiling and happy, being her usual self. At this time, Johnny was again a no-show. I asked her how her search went. She rushed over to my desk and said, 'We found a nice place not too far from the office.' 'We,' I asked. She smiled and said, 'Yes girl, Ayden will be coming with me. He said his wife is cheating on him and he is tired of putting up with it.' All I could say was WOW, but before I could get it out, HERE'S JOHNNY...

"When Johnny walked in, I almost did not recognize him. The hair on his face was disheveled and he looked like he had not slept in days. Screaming and yelling the first words out of his mouth:

"'You BITCH; you would leave me for that punk-ass nigger. He isn't worth nothing. I'm the best you would ever have. I have never done anything to hurt you. I gave you everything. You fucking snake.' It was so still in the office at that point. As he was yelling he was walking closer and closer to Brooke. She never even jumped. She stood her ground as to say, man please. I guess the black in me took over because I noticed I was under my desk when it got silent. I was afraid this dude had a gun or something. It was quiet enough for me to hear a door open to one of the supervisor's offices. I was hoping and praying that it was not Ayden. Thank God it wasn't. It was Brad."

Digital said, "Yeah, I know him. He has been with the company for 20 years plus."

"Brad came out cool, calm and collected. 'Johnny, come into my office. This is something you don't want to do right now.'"

"'Do I have to, I have not done anything yet, I'm just trying to have a conversation with MY WIFE.'"

"'I understand, but you seem a little tired and you are screaming at the top of your lungs as if she were deaf.' I could not see what was happening, but after what seems like hours, but only minutes, Johnny and Brad go into the office. You could hear all the folks on the floor whispering and looking and Brooke. I finally crawled out of my hiding place and walked over to Brooke's desk to make sure she was OK. She just had a smile on her face, like a plan was coming together. Another supervisor came out on the floor and asked us to get back to work. About 20 minutes after that, Brad and Johnny walked out of the office. Again, it was very still on the floor. Johnny made his way over to Brooke's desk and said, 'I will be out by next week. Can you please ride out the lease so that I don't lose my deposit?' Brooke looked at him and simple said, 'Nope!'

"Johnny's facial express went from sad to pitiful. I just felt so bad for him. How can you be with someone, all in love like there is no other person for you and then treat them like dirt? Johnny walked over to his desk and started to pack his personal items. I was really confused by this time. Did they fire him or did he quit? After Johnny left, the day went on as normal. I did see Ayden, but he was only there to meet Brooke for lunch."

"Man, that is some drama," Digital said. "So is that it? Is this *a to be* continued?"

"Well, I did find out that, lucky for Johnny, there was an opening in another city. He was able to transfer out and get a fresh start.

"So you are telling me this man left the state?"

"Yeah! I think it was for the best, I think he could have really hurt that girl. He looked like a crazy person that day. He transferred to the Chicago office. I heard he had family out there. Hopefully, he will get the support he needs to move past this mess.

"As for Ayden and Brooke, they are the new happy couple on the floor. I'm sure in the near future I will have an update on this story. I know Brooke was very competitive, but man she don't play."

"Do you think you could take her in a dog fight or even a fight for a job?" Digital asks.

"In a dog fight, NO, she plays dirty. In a fight for a job, I would say yes on paper. I'm better and more qualified than she is, but she knows how to work the right people to get what she needs. Right now, she has the advantage."

Digital did not say anything for a few minutes, so I decided to take a leap. "Babe, I did not mean anything about the pick earlier. I know I just hate that we had to deal with drama in our own marriage and from time to time, I think about it. It really hurts me and I just pray that one day we can truly move on."

He turns to the side facing me. As he turned I could smell he sweet but strong scent. "I know one-way you could make it up to me." He starts moving is body as if a fish out of water.

I said, "What, go swimming, sure we can do that this weekend."

As he was smiling he grabbed me by the waist and pulled me closer to him. Even through the sheets I could feel how hard he was. It does not take him long to get ready for me. All I had on was a t-shirt and some cute boy shorts I like to wear. They make my butt look big and juicy. "Take off your shirt," he asked. I obeyed, moving slow so that he would not get all the goods at one time. After throwing my shirt on the floor, I lie sideways facing him using the pillow to prop my head. I purposely cover my breast so that he would have a reason to find them. He is so gently when touching my body, only using his fingertips to caress my skin. Those touches make me so excited. I move with his touch. As he gets closer to me, his fingers go from my legs to my stomach to my butt. I know what he truly wants is to touch my breast, but he always saves the best for last. He kisses me on my neck and traces he touch to my breast. My nipples are hard and wanting to be touched. As his tongue dances around my nipples, my hand moves down his body until I find what's waiting for me. Just the slightest touch makes him shiver just a little. That was my sign that he liked it and wanted more. Digital was all man in the bedroom and my small hands could only make it halfway around his snake. That was enough to make him grab me by the neck and kiss me passionately.

As he was kissing me he worked his body on top of mine. I was just as excited as he was and he knew it even with my shorts still on. He teased me a few times, rubbing it against my clit. Then he was in me. The heat and strength from his body is like a rush. I came only a few seconds after he started to stroke, but I did not want him to stop. I have plenty more where that came from. He is like a big beast on top of me and is able to ride me and hold me tight without missing a step. We can go like this for hours. He controls himself and make his movements, so that I feeling every part of him. When he can no longer contain himself, his stokes are harder and deeper. My little hands are gripping his butt and making is knees weak. He leans downs to suck on my breast and in the moment we come together. He stretches himself out, grabbing my hips and moving my body in sync with his release. After we are done, he lies on my side holding me close, but never coming out of me. Lord, I love this man, please, continue to help us become strong within you. I say this to myself each night before I go to sleep. Good night, babe.

Chapter 5

The Stutter Man

A few weeks went by before Digital and I had any stories to share. He was very busy with work and he was coming home so late. There was a major leak off the Gulf Coast and a lot of the major oil companies were checking their contracts. His boss made him lead Project Manager over the contract reviews and he worked from sunup till sundown. As mom, I held down the house as best as I could. During his long days and long meetings, he comes across some very interesting people. The oil companies were sending representatives from all over the country to Digital's office. As in any meetings, after a while, people stop playing nice and their true colors come out. On this particular Thursday night, Digital arrived home around 9 p.m., and was so excited to have a night of conversation.

I let the kids stay up so that they could see him before they went to bed. Blake was a teenager and having is ups and downs in school. He needed the one-on-one guy time with Digital, so that he would not get out of control. "Isis, Blake come downstairs, dad will be home soon."

"Mom, is it still OK for me to talk to dad before I go to bed?" Blake asked.

"Sure baby, I told him you needed to have some man time. You sure I can't help?" Blake faced all but turned red and I had my answer. I smiled and said, "Don't worry about it." At that time, we heard the garage door opening and Digital's car pulling in. Isis, my sneaky child, decided to hide behind the sofa so that she could scare her dad as he walked in.

"BOO!!" Digital jumped and she sprang from the back of the sofa. "Girl, you almost scared me. Ha, ha, you thought you had me. I knew you were there." She made her famous scrunch mad face and pounced on him like a cat. "I scared you and I'm telling everybody."

"You what?" Digital started to tickle her until she confesses that she was not able to scare him. I love watching them play together. He is a big sissy around her. "OK, big head, it's time for bed." Isis gives him one big hug before she runs up the stairs. "Don't forget to say your prayers," I yelled. Blake was sitting on the sofa playing it cool. He stood up to give his dad that manly hug. My boys, what am I going to do with them?

"Dang boy, you are growing too fast." Blake smiled and said, "I know, I'm taller than mom now." That was very true. I noticed it a few days ago when we were hanging out in the kitchen. All I could think was that I would have to buy him some new clothes were soon. Darn kids!

At the front of the house Digital has a man cave with all of his sports memorabilia. With all his travels to sporting events and with the help of our parents, his room has the true feel of a real sports arena. This is also the spot of his and Blake's man time. I'm so glad that Digital takes time out with him like that. A lot of men would run away from another's man responsibility, but he never hesitated. They were in there for about an hour. I had already gone to the bedroom and was waiting for my alone time with my man. Blake came in the room and told me good night. I asked if he was better and he nodded his head in agreement. I could hear him running upstairs as Digital came into the room.

"Do you want anything to eat?"

"I'm good. One good thing about all these meetings is that we get great lunches and dinners. They also said that this would be the last late week. The President has finally sent in government officials to offer support and we have another department coming in to start the cleanup. Are you sleepy? I have a story for you."

"No, I'm good to go." Again, my goofy man was so eager to share his story, but he has to shower first. After about 30 minutes of showering and getting cleaned up, he opens the door naked and proud. I looked at him and said, "I'm going to put you on that pole and make us some extra money." He just laughs and jumps in the bed, running away from the cold air.

"OK, I want to say, it is not right to laugh at this story, but I just have to ask the Lord to forgive me because I cannot help it."

I was very curious now and ready for him. I was laying on my back with my head turned to him.

"During all this contract mess I think I told you that the company was bringing in all of these different reps to give their outlook of the situation. They did not all come at the same time, but after a week everyone that was due had arrived. The first guy that came was from Denver. He is a Hispanic man, average build and clean cut. He is very smart and one thing I notice about him was his eyes. He has bright green eyes. I'm not trying to check him out, but they look almost fake.

After he was brought in and got comfortable, you know me; I speak and try to be cool with folks. He name was Cody, but what threw me off was that he had a speech problem. I just thought it would be weird that a company would send a rep out who had an issue like that. He stuttered, but I did notice that he did his best to control it when he was on the hot seat. After hanging with him for a few days, I did notice that Cody did not show any signs of stuttering when a sexy lady was around."

I chuckled at the thought. "So I guess if you are not a hot chick, you knew by his reaction."

Digital smiled and said, "That is so true. There is a one lady in the office I call home boy. She dresses and acts just like a dude. It takes Cody five minutes to say hi."

By this time we were both laughing. Now I see why he asked for forgiveness. That's just not right.

"Cody is really cool and I notice he keeps close to me during the meetings. He arrived on Monday. That same week on Thursday more representatives were arriving and one guy was named Kyle. He's a big ole black dude. Look like Vin Rains in a suite. Kyle was out of the military and you could tell by the way he carried himself. He likes to follow orders and give them. On the back side, this dude also stuttered. I was shocked asking myself, 'what's really going on?' The day that Kyle arrived, Cody was in another meeting and they did not get to meet. I thought it was weird, but did not think anything more about it. We had so many reps come in that it is not strange that they did not run into each other right away. By Friday, we were all tired and frustrated. Not getting any support from management and then being placed in a room with a ton of guys that think they know everything does not help."

"I'm sure you are one of those bullies."

He smiled and said, "Hell, they are coming to my house, they should show some respect." I just rolled my eyes. "Anyway, the last meeting of the day, we are trying to resolve one particular issue on trying not to spike gas prices and trying to make sure the company does not take a low financial blow. In this meeting everyone is in one room. Cody, as always, is in the chair next to me. Kyle is sitting across from us. Jack, one of the vice presidents, opens up the floor to comments. Military Kyle is the first to speak."

"Aaagain, my my my name is Kyle. Weeee cannot make a a a determination oooon the the the financial is is is situation unless weeee ha, ha have all the numbers."

"Digital, you a fool," is all I can say and trying my best to contain my laughter.

"I look over at Cody and this dude looks pissed. Before I can swing my chair over and asked him if he was OK, all hell broke loose. Mumumumu mother fucker, wh, wh, wh, why are you ma ma ma marking me. Wh, wh, wh, who told you that I, I, I, I stutter. It it it it not fu, fu, fu, funny bi, bi, bi, bitch! Oh my God is the look I had on my face. I just realized that this is the first time that these dudes are being introduced. Cody did not know that Kyle had a speech impediment."

I was on the floor laughing at this point. "Wait, wait, are you telling me this dude cuss this man out in a meeting? I'm not ready; I have to catch my breath."

Once I started to laugh, Digital was right there with me. We both had tears on our eyes. I just could not image that happening. This could not be true. Once we both calmed down, Digital tried his best to finish his story, but he was hard.

"Cody and Kyle was both standing at this point and coming around the table. Kyle was cussing back at him because the whole situation caught him off guard. We have the two reps and the VP's trying to get in the middle of them." Kyle finally was able to say, 'He, he, he, hey man, I'm no, no, no, not trying to, to, to, make fu, fu, fu, fun of you. I, I, I, I, I stutter, too.' I finally got Cody's attention and told him that he was telling the truth. I just told him, we had been so busy that I did not think anything about it. The VPs let the misunderstanding go and just told us all to take a break and we will meet on Monday. Cody and I went back to my desk and he was explaining to me how he was teased so much that Kyle caught him off guard. By this time Kyle was walking up and they both apologized to each other. After Kyle walked away I asked Cody, why when there is a sexy lady around, he does not stutter? All he could say was, 'ba, ba, ba, ba, bad, bi, bi, bitches makes me me, me, me nervous.'" I was done.

"Digital that was a good one, where do you find these people?" He smiles and said, "They find me."

What a way to end our night.

"By the way, Cody has been here for three weeks now so I have more to share, but I will save it for our next go around." Before I could say OK, Digital was calling the hogs. I'm not sure how I sleep through that. My poor boo was so tired.

Night babe.

Chapter 6

African Queen

As the weeks goes by our story sharing gets left in the cold due to football season. Digital is a true sports fan. When he finds a superstar he likes, he sticks with that person even when he is not performing per the millions of dollars that this person was being paid. Digital often travels to see his favorite players at live games. Him and a few buddies traveled to Florida to watch his team win eight straight and secure a seat in the playoffs. He was so happy that he was at that game because it was considered the comeback of the century. To make sure we don't miss too much of our time, we'd start our talks a little earlier during the day when the seasons change from boring (nothing on TV) to ESPN everyday all-day season. I don't mind, that is something that he enjoys and I will never take that away from him.

"Hey babe, you remember a few months ago when I told you the story about the stuttering couple?" I had to laugh at the thought of that story. "Yes, why do you ask?"

"Well, I have a part two." On that note I was immediately interested. It was the weekend and college football did not start until that afternoon. We were just lying in the bed talking about random things when he started his story.

"In the stuttering story I told you about Military Kyle and Denver Cody. A few weeks after their pow-wow all of the contract issues had been resolved and everyone went back to their respected cities. Cody, however, decides that he loved this city and wanted to stay. Cody is around our age, but he does not have any kids so making a move like that would not be so hard to do. After he had a few meetings with leadership to secure a job in my office, we worked together to make sure he planned as best as he could so that he would not run into too many bumps in the road. At first he was looking at apartments, but he found a very nice subdivision on the north side of Austin. We took a ride out there one day on lunch to make sure this is something he really wanted to do. Have you heard of the subdivision River Stone? It is not too far from downtown."

"Yes, I have a few co-workers that have purchased homes out there. It is very nice."

"I thought so, too. On the day that we traveled to see the homes, they were having an inventory blow-out sale. The sales representative was more than happy to show Cody what she had left in stock. At first she was showing us four and five bedroom homes. Don't get me wrong very nice, but this is a single man with no kids. Cody was just going alone with her and I finally had to say something. You know me, she was working my nervous and you know my patience gets really short really fast." That I know. "So I told her that he is just looking for a small, one-level house to get started in. She looked at Cody for approval like I did not know what I was talking about. He finally agrees with me and she finally decided to show us what he had asked for. I truly believe that if I was not there, that boy would have purchased a big-ass house.

"A few weeks went by before the sale was final and Cody was all moved in. His family from Denver helped him move in. Before I forget, he is having a house-warming party and he wants us to come."

"What kind of house did he buy again?"

"It is a one-level, three bedroom house. When you walk in, you enter a foyer. There is a dining room that he said he will make his office. Off the dining room is a bedroom and a full bath. The house is open, which makes is look very big. He has a huge family room, which connects with the kitchen. Buying an inventory home was a bonus because he was able to get all the nice upgrades, such as granite countertops and hardwood floors. In the back of the house is another smaller bedroom and the master bedroom with a full bath. The builder did a great job of using the space in the house. They gave a good deal that he could not pass up. It was originally priced at $180,000 but because it was an inventory home and had been sitting for about six months, he closed at $143,000 plus a two-year warranty on any issues that may occur."   "Wow, that is a great deal. We should get him a gift card so that he could buy what he really needs."

"Yeah, that will work. So he is all settled and really enjoying the city when I find out the true reason for him moving down. What is one reason a man will change his style of living?"

I smiled and said, "For some kitty cat."

"EXACTLY!"

"When you were telling the story of Brooke and Ayden, I immediately thought of Zabrina. She is what some guys call our 'African Queen.' Don't get jealous, but I have to say, she is a bad chick. She has the looks, the walk, the talk, everything, but she has a messed up attitude. I heard someone say once; she looks great on the outside, but is rotten to the core. That's Zabrina. We call her Za. She moved here from Nigeria when she was a little girl."

Before Digital could move forward with his story I asked, "Do you care to share some details on this bad chick Mr. Man?" He smiled and said, "Don't get jealous."

"I'm not, but I like to see what you consider BAD." He chuckled and begins to describe her. "For a chick she is pretty tall. I think she is 6 foot, 1. She has dark skin, but it has a red tint to it. You can tell that she takes really good care of herself. Her skin looks almost perfect. She keeps her hair in braids, but it is very long. She has an African accent, but not that heavy so it makes her voice cute; it's not hard to understand her. And, of course, she has a big juicy booty and big boobs."

I took the pillow and hit him in the face. "What, you never said if I look it was cheating."   "Well, today I'm making a new rule. Looking is cheating."

Digital turns on his side and said "trust me; you don't have anything to worry about. She looks good, I give her that, but she is just so darn fake. One day she will come in and tell me good morning and the next day she will walk right past me like I was a ghost. I will never do anything to hurt out family."

I grabbed him by the face and tried to give him a kiss. He turned his head and said," you have not brushed your teeth yet." Again, pillow to the face.

"Za is the office administrator so she is not making as much as the rest of us. I think she has a second job. When I said she reminded me of Brooke, I was thinking of how they choose to use people, men in particular to get what they want. Za flirts with all the guys and from what I heard most of them have run through her. What she does not like about the situation is that she is trying to find someone to take care of her and all these dudes in the office treat her like a ho. That is until Cody came into the picture. As a guy, I have a duty to give any new comers the law of the land. Let them know who's married, single, a freak, etc..."

"And how would you know she is a freak?" He had that deer caught in the headlights look and said, "Did I say freak?" That deserved a pillow to the face. "Anyway, I did give Cody a heads up about this chick, but it went in one ear and out the other. It started with the flirting and the lunches in the break room. The guys and I would sit in there and talk about them. Saying that it should not take Cody long to tap that ass."

I was laughing and shaking my head at the same time. "What we did not know was that Cody was a mark and he was forming true feelings for this girl. Za knew she had him. She was always building him up all the time.

"Now that Cody is all moved in I decided to take him to lunch to see where his head was at. I asked him how serious it was with Za and how did he plan on going with her? Cody was so excited that someone seemed interested in his new relationship. He smiled and said, 'Man, she is the girl of my dreams.' Don't forget, Cody stutters and our conversation always takes longer than a normal one."

Digital is so crazy; I had to laugh at the thought. "Ma, ma, ma, ma man, sh, sh, sh she, said sh, sh, sh, she love me too! Sh, sh, sh, sh said she ha, ha, ha never been treated li, li, li like this be, be, be before."

"Digital stop, you are so stupid, just tell the story."

"What, I thought you wanted the full effect?"

"If you give me the full effect, you will miss kick-off." With that he stopped messing around. I have to say it is very funny. I have to make sure I don't laugh in anyone's face when I actually meet them. "Cody had plenty more to tell me about Za and their relationship.

"'Man Digital, she told me that the guys in the office treat her so bad and she was nervous about hooking up with me. I let her know that I was not like everyone else. Digital, it has always been hard for me to find a girl or excuse me a lady who respected me and did not care about my disability. She told me she did not care about that. She also told me she was struggling to pay her bills and was working two jobs. I decided to move her in with me. I want to do it before the party so that my family could meet her and that she was comfortable.'"

All I could say was *wow!*

"You should have seen my face. I try to keep a blank look, but I guess I had the look of horror on my face because Cody asked me what was wrong? I had to break it down for him again. Cody, the guys in the office treats her like they do because she uses people. She always has her hand out. There are time when she can be so nice and then other times when she treats people like dirt. She even treats me like that and I don't do anything to that darn girl. Second, a lot of the guys in the office have run through her. She is not some virgin queen like you are painting her out to be. Man, she is only using you because you are a nice guy. I thought I hurt his feelings. In a way I wanted to because he was doing great things and I just wanted to look for him. He finally said, 'I know about the guys in the office. She told me that she was just looking for love in all the wrong places. This is something I want and I want you to be happy for me.'" I asked him, "Do you think your family will have issues with her and the fact that you are moving her in so fast?"

He said his mom is very protective, but they have spoken to each other on the phone and my mom is starting to really like her.

"That girl is a good thing. Getting in good with the mom always helps. So you know what, I left it alone. He is a grown man and I just hope she does not hurt him too bad. I just told him to watch his money and don't give her the world until he is 100 percent sure she is there for him. Now babe, listen how she answers this million dollar question. I asked Cody with all this love talk and moving her in with him, has he hit it yet? I know he may sound crude, but that is a guy thing."

To be honest I was very curious about that answer as well. I was thinking he put it on her good or at least the other way around for him to act like she was the only girl on the planet. "Well, what did he say?" By this point I had my pillow in a choke hold. Digital shook his head from side to side and said, "No. This girl told him she stopped sleeping with guys and made a vow not to sleep with anyone until she was married. The sad thing about it, I know for a fact that one of the representatives from California hit that before he went back home after our contract negations."

"So I guess you are not going to let Cody in on that juicy detail."

"Nope, he said it, he is a grown-ass man and he will have to figure this out for himself."

Man that is crazy, we see stuff like this happening all the time on TV or in the lives of some superstars, but to have it up close and personal, that is just crazy. I start worrying about people in that type of situation. What if she runs off with his money? Digital has already tried to warn him and he is right, he cannot force his hand. "So when is the house-warming party?" Digital was getting out the bed and getting ready for his sports-filled day. "It is next weekend. It is early in the day so we can go hang out for a few hours. I will pick up a gift card for him next week, just remind me."

I looked over at the clock and it was way past 10 a.m. Wow, we were lazy today. As I got up from the bed there was a knock at our door. I already knew who it was. "Come in little lady." She laughed and said, "How did you know it was me?" Before I could answer, Digital said "because we could see that big head coming from a mile away." Perfect way to get my day started.

Chapter 7

Girl Fight

Like most companies, some are in the process of downsizing, sending business overseas, closing or merging. My company just went through a merger and acquired a new business in whole. We took over people's assets and policies. I knew big changes were coming because our leaders were making room for more people to start working in our office very soon. The break- room doubled in size. Vending machines and a whole new kitchen area was added, along with additional tables and chairs. Updated flat-screen televisions were a final touch. Funny, no one has the remote to change to channels. Leadership chooses to keep it on CNN all day. New cubicals were also added to accommodate everyone. A week before the newbies were due to arrive, they held a big meeting with each team letting us know as many ins and outs they cared to shared. I remember looking over at Brooke and Ayden. Six months has gone by since the fight with her ex-husband on the job and they still seem like the happy couple. I laughed at the thought.

Kathy, our soft-spoken Director of Operations led the conversation. "As you all know, we are taking over Rock, Inc. This merger and all of the contract negations have been finalized. I'm sure and hope that most of you have been following all the changes on the news or even in the company newsletter. As a company we try our best to keep all of you informed."

I took a deep breath at that thought. Some companies can really be full of shit. Just last month, our vice president paid us a lovely visit and informed us of all the success that the company was having. We were making money and everyone's jobs were safe from all the economic issues that were plaguing other companies. It is so nice how they pay this team a visit using company money for all their first-class tickets and first-class hotel rooms. Driving up to the office in a very expensive car and Lord, don't let anyone be parked in their parking spot, all hell will break loose. They walk in with tailored suits and when I ask for a raise it is as if I'm speaking a foreign language. At the time I was relived at that thought. Two weeks went by and the company had a mass layoff, so much for honesty and integrity. Our office only lost two people, but countrywide, we lost over 100. I later found out that negations in other countries were successful as well and a ton of business was transferred overseas. Now we have had a quote unquote successful merger. I just don't get it.

"With this merger we are adding 25 people to this office. We are setting up training classes so that the individuals coming in not only understand the policy and procedures of this company, but also have an understanding of our office flow. Please make sure that you stay on top of your day-to-day duties, as I know with all the distractions it can bring low production. Please welcome all the acquired people from the merger with open arms. Does anyone have any questions?"

I looked around the room and I could tell that folks really did not have a care in the world about all the new changes. As long as they had a job they were AOK. The leaders just don't get the fact that the layoff really hurt morale. "I do have a question Kathy,"

Brooke spoke up. "With all the new arrivals, will there be any new job titles forming such as training mangers or supervisors?" The queen of power has spoken. I have to give it to her; she is always so stunning and professional.

"Yes, Brooke and as soon as those jobs are available, which should be by the end of this week, we will send out a mass communications to everyone. Human Resources will do the job matches and we will conduct interviews in the office to all that qualify."

What Kathy was saying is that yes we will send out an e-mail to everyone to make sure we are within the company's guidelines, but we pretty much know who we want in those positions and if they apply they will get it. Brooke smiled and said, "Thanks Kathy, looking forward to receiving that e-mail."

"Any more questions?" The room went silent. "OK, back to work."

As I walked back to my desk, Brooke was already there waiting on me. "Girl, are you going to apply for any of the new jobs that they may post? You know I will jump on any opportunity to better myself."

That I DO know. I smiled and said, "Maybe, it just depends on some factors like who I will report to, pay and time out of my already busy life."

"You know a family always slows down success. I don't have time for it right now. I have to get what's mine. I had to set Ayden straight on that really fast. Doing the *I want your baby song and dance.* "Really, what about his family? Is he still married?"

"Yes, and that bitch is always acting a fool. She calls and texts his phone all the time, always asking for money. We almost had a fight because she wants to pop up at my place talking about that we need to pay her rent because he left her high and dry. She better get a job. I'm not the one. After screaming back and forth he was finally able to get her to leave. I told him he needs to drop her really fast. You see how fast I had Johnny running."

I had not thought about him in a while. "How is Johnny?"

"He is fine; I go up to see him every now and then. Get me some quick dick. Sometimes I forget how sexy he is and how great in bed he is. You know I'm a diva, but there are times when I need that right person to fulfill all my needs. I taught Johnny well and he has not missed a beat."

"How do you manage to get him to see you, I would think he would not want anything to do with you after what happened."

"I'm sexy, I know how to work my mouth and not with just words. Have him melting just like candy."

I think if I were white, my face would be hot red. I already have a vivid imagination, so her storytelling does not help.

"Of course that is between you and me. I know Ayden still fucks his wife. He said he doesn't, but I'm far from stupid. So this is like payback until he gets his shit together."

I must have had a look of wow on my face because all she could do is laugh at me. Some of the folks on our row were looking back so she walked to her desk, still laughing. That darn girl is a mess. I sent her a quick instant message and said, you *don't have to worry about me spreading your business, but please be careful.* She shot back, *I know, that is why I don't mind telling you anything. Stuff I tell you, I never hear it repeated compared to some of these B.... And yes, always be careful. I* closed out the message and finished up my work for the day.

A few weeks later, the new faces started to arrive. In a business office, you will always have more females than males, but this lot was about even. It was a pretty good mixture of cultures and races. I liked that. I really like to get to know different people. Right before the new folks started to arrive, the e-mail was sent with the new job postings. The only listings were for a supervisor, team leader and trainer. Brooke and I put in for the jobs and just as I figured, they had already pinpointed who they wanted in those positions. How funny life can be. It is like you know what is going on, but because they are so slick about it, there is really no room to complain to Human Resources. Oh well, I know that when something comes up for me, I will get it. Brooke, on the other hand, was truly pissed. I think she was more pissed at Ayden because she figures she could use him as leverage to pull the supervisor job. She is learning that she picked the wrong one to help move her up. Karma is a bitch sometimes.

The leaders never did an official meet and greet with all of the new faces. So me being me, I take it upon myself to introduce myself to the folks I run into. Most of them are very young and ready to run with the company. I remember when I had that same drive. After a company let's you down so many times, that drives seems to get lost and you find yourself happy to just work and go home. One of the new ladies I ran into was what my husband would call *Butch*. Her name was Ross. She was a small lady, not only in height, but in size as well, but with a nice- sized chest. Her hair is jet-back and she had it cut short like a crew cut. Blues eyes and a cute smile, but bated for the other team. It was no secret that she was a lesbian. She was not ashamed of that fact and I respect her for that and for the fact that she was not hitting on me. Ross had a very strong Southern accent. Very close to being a redneck. For some reason, it suited her just fine. She tried to mix it with a down South thug tone so it was funny to listen to her speak.

Another new chick was named Tamia. She was a thick black woman with a huge chest. . She also had long black hair that she would keep in a bun. She was also very tall. Taller than me for sure and I had good height for a woman. When I would see her I just thought to myself, *man her back has to be killing her. She has a lot to support*. She was super religious. Some would say she is a Holy Roller. She is quick to spread the good word and quick to judge. I do believe and trust in God, but I'm not slapping folks with the bible. Putting Tamia and Ross together was a bomb waiting to go off. Neither one of them is afraid to express their opinion. Tamia would comment to other folks in the office how Ross was living a life of sin because of her lifestyle. She thinks she can have a sit down and make her see the light. I had to shake my head at the thought. Some folks should really just mind their own business.

After all the new folks were trained and working on the floor I notice that the Tamia and Ross cubical were across from each other. How funny is that? Each lady had their own click of works friends; so for the most part, they did not have to really communicate with each other unless it was work related. It seems to be working out well, so my initial concerns died down until, of course, that fateful day arrived.

A month had gone by and Brooke was at my desk while we were taking a break. "Girl, that chick Tamia is a mess. She keeps going on how Ross is a sinner and sitting that close to her is bringing over evil spirits."

"Are you serious, I know she didn't?"

"Yes, I hope if they do get into a fight, so I'm close-by to cheer Ross on."

"Brooke, you are so stupid. Hey, I heard there are some new job openings coming our way. Hopefully it is something we can jump on and improve our walk up this corporate ladder."

"Yeah, I will check into it also. I'm tired of what I'm doing now. I'm getting very bored with it."

As we were talking we decided to head to the break room. Our leaders are treating the office to lunch and we wanted to get in there before it got too crowed. Looking ahead, I could see Ross. We caught up with her to see how her day was going.

"What's up Ross? Running to the break room I see."

"Hello ladies. My day is going very well. I'm more excited about tonight. I have a hot date with this bad chick."

I had to smiled, not only listening to her speak in that Southern accent, but to see her reaction to what she would call a bad chick. I knew Digital's views, but I was very curious as to what she liked. Call me crazy.

"Ross, you will have to take us out with you sometime," Brooke noted. "I heard you know how to have a good time."

She smiled "call me party central. Come out with me anytime. I think both of you are really cool, unlike some of these other hos that work here." As she was talking we were entering the break room. Tamia was there and I knew who Ross was referring to. I gave Tamia a smile to greet her as I walked over to the line to get our free lunch. I don't think she even saw my gesture because she was so focused on Ross. Ross and Brooke were behind me still chatting about folks. They cut their conversation down to a whisper at this point, so I could not really focus on it. You could feel the atmosphere in the room change. Tamia and her click of holy rollers at their table with their food. Their conversation also was toned down to whispers. As I was about to turn to Brooks and Ross try to do something to spruce up something in the break room, Ross's phone rings.

"What's up? WHAT! Hold on, let me call you back. Chani, I'm going to make a call outside, just in case anyone is looking for me. It's a personal matter."

"Sure, I will make sure they know where you are. Take your time." Ross quickly exited the break room and took the side door where usually the smokers would hang out on their break. The company tried to promote a smoke-free environment, but if you have a habit you will find a place to take a quick puff. So they created a nice space on the side of the building out of view of visitors. Ross had to have been gone for no more than five minutes when I notice Tamia getting up from her group and heading out the door. I watch her take the side exit also.

"Brooke, I think Tamia is about to confront Ross. She just went out the side door and I know she is not a smoker."

"Man I hope she is not going to mess with that girl today. It seemed like that phone call was nothing nice and I'm sure she would not be in the best of places to deal with someone wanting to lay hands on her. Let's take a walk and make sure everything is OK."

We grabbed our food and quickly brought it to our desk. After that we took the side door to make sure that Ross and Tamia were OK. I have never been out this exit. I could not believe how thick the smoke was compared to our smoke-free environment. Man, I could not stand that smell. Brooke was in front of me going down the stairs to the final exit and she was not moving fast enough. When we reached the door, I did not have time to take a break. Drama was already in the works. At first, all I could hear was Ross cussing out someone and I knew who that someone was.

"Bitch, what the fuck is your problem? You don't know anything about me and the way I live. You don't have the right to judge me about anything. I bet I know that Bible better than you."

"Even the Devil knows the Bible."

"Why the hell do you care how I live? If you were this great woman of God, you are supposed to pray for me and keep it moving."

"I have tried to pray for you many times, but you just blew me off. Ross, this is about your soul. If you keep fornicating with women, you will go to hell."

I saw Ross ball her hand up and move towards Tamia very fast. Tamia was sitting, not taking the situation seriously at all, but as Ross approached her, she stood. She hugged her Bible as if she were hugging a man. I really think she wanted Ross to hit her, but that was not happening on my watch. Brooke and I ran over to where they were and got in the middle before it got any worse than what it already was. I was facing Ross, and Brooke took on Tamia. "What are the problem ladies," I asked. Looking at Ross, I could clearly see that she was beyond pissed off. Ross looked at me and said in a voice that was just to calm for someone that looked so upset.

"This bitch came out here while I was in the middle of a very important conversation and threw holy water on me. Then she attempted to cast out my 'so-called' demons." All I could do was shake my head.

"Tamia, what is your deal; why would you do something like that?" She took a deep breath as if she did not think she had to explain herself, but the look Brooke was giving her suggested that she better answered my question or she will have more than just Ross to deal with. "My intentions were to come out here and have a simple talk with Ross. It is my obligation under God's word that I spread the good news and let her know she is living a life of sin." As she was telling her side of the story, I had to gently restrain Ross because I could feel her muscle tighten up as I placed my hands on her arms. "When I did get outside, she was on the phone screaming at someone on the other end, using words that I cannot repeat. I started to turn around and let her finished because I could tell that she was very upset. The Holy Spirit told me not to be afraid of the Devil and to continue with my mission. I knew the only way to get her attention was to just start with the holy water."

I was truly in awed by this conversation. Again, folks' life styles, religion whatever is their business, but I truly think she over-stepped her boundaries. I think I would have knocked her out also, throwing water on, me. I had to reassess myself and make sure that I speak without choosing sides. "Tamia, our company does not discriminate on race, color, age, national origin, disability. That same statement also includes sex and religion. If Ross does not want you to speaking or judge her on the way she lives her life, then you need to keep it moving. You pray for her in your own way."

"You know Tamia; I would have kicked your ass if you would have thrown water on this body," Brooke had to make a statement. "I understand how you feel. I grew up in a very religious household, but I had to make my own way. Right now Chani and I will not report this to leadership, but you ladies better get it together or it will be reported and we will let them handle per company policy. I'm sure both of you need a job at this point. I don't care if you do or don't say you're sorry to each other. What better happen is that you get back on the floor, get to work and not a word of this is to be repeated. Understand?"

Tamia, not understanding that she would have gotten her ass kicked if we had not come outside, said *yes* very quickly and headed to the door. Ross nodded her head in agreement, but sat down on the benches set up in the small courtyard. Besides it being an area for smokers, I never realized how pretty this space was. Thank God no one else was outside when this happened. This would have been very bad. Looking over to Ross, she was shaking. "You OK?" She coughed to clear her throat. "Yes, I'm good. She just caught me off guard. I was on the phone with my roommate and she said that she thinks that the girl I brought over stole some money from her. She was bitching at me about it and I'm not one to back down. Then Tamia comes out here with that bullshit."

Ross had to chuckle. "I knew she had a plan of attacked, but dam did she pick a bad time." Brooke was shaking her head and said, "Well it is over with now. Get yourself together and come on back in. If you feel it is still some tension, let us know and we will see if you can take half the day off." Again shaking her head in agreement, she said thank you.

Brooke and I headed back to the office. As soon as we made in through the doors we had to laugh. "I knew something was going down. That dam Tamia is nothing nice." I was just laughing because I just could not believe that someone would really go that far. When we made it through the main office door, we made sure we were had our work faces back on. We walked to our desk and as we past the aisle I could see Tamia at her desk working. I guess she took Brooke's threat serious. Hell, I would have. Brooke is something else and with her friends in high places, not telling what she is really capable of. I never saw Ross come back in, but knew she would be. As I sat made my way to my desk, I replayed the recent events in my head one more time to makes sure I had the details correct. What a story I had for Digital.

Chapter 8

New House Smell

Digital had to remind me about Cody's housewarming party. I was very excited to meet Cody and his family. I was also interested in seeing the infamous Zabrina. As I prepared myself for a nice day out, I thought about our night together. All of our talks are so much fun. We laugh together and at times have some very serious conversations about our stories. After telling Digital about Tamia and the Holy Roller gang, we had to think about our religious lifestyle. Since moving back home, I have bounced around to a few churches not really finding what we had back home. I finally settled on one that was very close to our home. They had areas for each of the kids so that they could learn God's word in their own prospective. After leaving church we will all take time out to discuss what we learned in church.

Unfortunately, Digital was not a part of these conversations. He is so much in love with his church back home, he just feels that he does not get what is needed out of any of the churches we have attended. I do come home afterwards and let him know what we talked about and how I feel about it and he listens. After listening to my Holy Roller story, he made a decision to start coming to church with us. "I'm the man of the house and I really need to show leadership in all aspects, not just financially or emotionally. I will be there with yall so that we can grow in the word together." I was so happy to hear him say that. I try not to bug him about it, but I do poke the bear from time to time. I guess my thought put a smile on my face as I was getting dressed. "Hey sexy, what's on your mind?"

"Actually, I was thinking about you and about how you want to grow strong in your walk with Christ. It is funny that Holly Roller did have an impact on someone." He smiled and grabbed me from behind, making sure I could feel how hard and warm he was. "If that makes you smile, let me show you how I can make you scream for joy."

"We have to go or we will be late." His smile went to a smirk and said, "Never put me first." I rolled my eyes and went to the closet to pick out a cute sundress to wear. One thing I love about Texas, its summer all year-round.

I like neutral colors. They just look so nice against my skin. There was a knock on the door and we already knew that the gang was looking for us. Digital went to the door, "who is it?" A shy voice almost at a whisper said "Isis." Digital opened the door to see his baby girl. She was all dolled up in a lavender sundress with silver sandals to match. He picked her up and gave her a big hug. Then he pretended to almost drop her. "Man that big head is so heavy." She smiled and cut her eyes down to a sliver and said, "I don't have a big head, but you do." It's just part of their ongoing fight, so cute. "Your momma is in the bathroom."

I was finishing up with my makeup and had the curling iron ready to make her look just as good as mom. "Momma, are you ready to comb my hair?"

"Yep, come on in sister." She skipped in and I began working my magic. Once I was done I had her hair tied up with candy canes flowing down her back. A cute bang to finish her off and she was good to go. I do the momma check to make sure that she follows what I think are the correct steps of grooming. I check eyes, ears, teeth and skin for dryness. I always have to double check Blake's lips because they are always super dry. He is getting older and is taking care of himself better, but I still have to check.

"Get your brother for me, you are good to go." She skipped away and Digital asked if we were ready to go. I nodded as I completed my final steps of looking my best. Blake walked in and I gave him a once over to make sure he looked good also. Typical teenagers dress up. Baggy jeans, sports logo t-shirt, baseball cap and tennis shoes to match. I just shook my head and said, "You look nice, let your dad know we are ready." We loaded up in his car and were on our way.

It took us about 45 minutes to get to Cody's home. The drive was really nice. I love the city. Both kids have a Smartphone, so they play games while Digital listened to his favorite songs on his iPod. I always have a book in hand and I was working on the Riley Jensen series. I really love this book and Riley, the lead character. They do movies on the Twilight and Harry Potter series; man, I wish someone would pick this up. As we pulled into the subdivision I take note of the beautiful manmade lakes. They were set up behind each home and each home had a small boat dock attached. Some homes had paddle boats and others had Jet Skis. There were also ducks swimming in the water. "Wow, this is really lovely." Isis asked if she could go out on a paddle boat.

"I'm not sure if Mr. Cody had one baby," Digital said. The automatic look of defeat was on her face so fast, I had to smile and say "maybe daddy can take us to a water park over the summer and you can have all the fun you want. Digital rolled his eyes, but Isis was back in happy land. Digital drove through the neighborhood with precision. He made a few turns and finally we were at Cody's home. We had to park down the street because the cars were lined up.   "Man how many folks did this boy invite? I see a lot of cars from the guys at work. You know they are only here to be nosy." I chuckled "well at least they will give us something to talk about later. We finally found a parking space about three houses down. Isis and I were in the lead and the boys were not too far back messing around. I turned to look back at them and Digital had Blake in a headlock. I just shooked my head. "Y'all stop playing!" Digital said it was Blake and Blake said he started it. Boys! As we approached the house I admired the landscape. There was a medium-size palm tree in the front yard and a curvy pathway that lead to a small porch. The porch was big enough for the black iron table and chair Cody had placed. Isis rang the doorbell and when Cody made it to the door we were all standing together.

"Hey family, come on in. Welcome, welcome." I had to turn off the laughter bug very quickly. I forgot just that fast that Cody stuttered and it almost caught me off guard. Cody, this is my wife Chani, my son Blake and my daughter Isis."

"Wow, he looks like mom and she looks like dad. Y'all come on in and make yourself at home. There is food in the kitchen. Blake, in the room to your right, there are boys back there playing video games. Sorry Isis, no little girls just yet."

"Mom, is it OK, can I go?" I nodded and he was gone before I could nod again. As we were making our way through the house and through the crowd, Digital would stop and speak to guys he knew from the job. Cody would stop and introduce us to his family. The house was very beautiful like Digital had described. The first room had been turned into an office. There was a very nice glass desk that his computer rested on. There were very nice shelves for his books and paperwork. He did not have a dining room table so it made the room look very large. There were chairs lined up against the walls so that everyone was comfortable. In the family room, he had a black wrap around sofa that could seat at least 10 people. There was a matching recliner, coffee table and side tables to match.

A child was sitting in the recliner and Cody went over to get him out. He offered it to me and Isis and I gladly accepted it. Digital and Cody walked back to the other room and start chatting it up with other co-workers. After I got comfortable in the chair I mustered up some courage and started to chat with the other ladies sitting on the sofa. They were all pretending to watch something on the TV, but they had it muted. "Hello ladies, I'm Chani, a friend of Cody's, how are you all doing today."

That got the ball rolling. A very beautiful lady spoke up first and said, "I think we are all great. My husband did the same thing with me as yours did. Drop me off and ran off to have fun. I'm Melanie by the way, Levi's wife."

"Oh, OK, Digital has mentioned Levi a few times."

"You know I tell Levi, we should all go out as couples, get to know each other."

"Now that is a great idea, I work a lot also and having to come home to kids each day, I tend to forget I need fun time as well."

All the ladies nodded in agreement. Before we could go deeper into our conversation a voice from behind me said, "So you are Digital's wife." It was as if the speaker was surprised and it almost ticked me off. I instantly knew who it was, Zabrina. Her African accent was stronger than Digital had mentioned. She walked over and said, "Digital speaks very highly of you. I thought you were Queen Elizabeth how he made you out to be."

"Well, I'm his queen. I take it you are Zabrina, correct? He has mentioned you maybe once."

Melanie looked at me as if to ask, *what's this bitch's problem?* "I'm Za, nice to finally meet you."

She put her hand out and I shook it very firmly as my dad has always taught me to. "Dang girl, you shake hands like a man."

"Sorry about that, my dad taught me to always be the aggressor."

"Is that how you got a man like Digital?" I had to instantly bite my lip. Melanie said, "Za, looks like you have really been hitting up the margarita machine haven't you?"

She smiled and said, "I'm sorry Chani, I'm a little tipsy. No harm, not foul."

I gave her my best fake smile and worked on changing the conversation back to focus on the party.

"So Za, how did all the moving go, the house is beautiful?"

"Yeah, I know. I'm great at stuff like that. Cody is so nice, he lets me do and spend what I want. I was able to make sure the house looked awesome for this party. You ladies know what I mean; I just can't be in a house that does not have any pizzazz."

"I personally take on one project at a time. I like to take my time and make sure I'm getting what I want," Melanie mentioned

"So what you are trying to say." It was clear the Za was on the defense. Melanie looked at her and gave her glaring look. "Look, I'm just letting you know how I would do it. I really think you need to stop drinking before you show your ass."

Za was already moving towards Melanie. Melanie and I stood up at the same time. I looked at Isis and told her to go get her dad. I did not want her to see a bunch of woman act a fool. I was looking at Melanie and saw even though she was clearly pissed off; she had a graceful glamour about herself with long wavy blonde hair and bright green eyes. She was a little shorter than I was, but she stood her ground. No booty, poor thing, but a nice-size chest. She had very thin red lips and as I got closer to her, I could tell she did not have on any lipstick. She was just a natural beauty. I made a move so that I was standing side-by-side with Melanie.

"Za, we are all cool here. We are just trying to get to know everyone. Please don't take our comments out of context. Cody is your man and his family is here, let's not make a scene." I did what I could to stall until Digital made it over to the family room. As he walked up he placed an arm over Melanie and my shoulders. "How is it going ladies?"

"Mr. Digital, we are great just making small talk." Za's tune had completely changed. She looked as innocent as a church mouse. He looked at me, "Babe, let's get something to eat." We walked over to the kitchen together and helped ourselves to all the food Cody and Za had for the party. I noticed outside he had tables and chairs set up on the patio and I instructed Isis to head that way. Digital was right behind us.

"So what was all of that about?" I looked at him as if I were searching for some hidden answers. "I know you said she was a mess, but I did not know she was borderline crazy. When she realized I was your wife she acted like I was not good enough for you. She said that you boost me up like I was the Queen of England. Who says that? Melanie tried to change the conversation and she got all snotty with her. As soon as you walked over she was all sweet and innocent."

"I told you that girl has problems."

"Does she want you are something?"

"She wants anything that can help her situation out."

"Well, I hope she calms down, she is really about to show out in front of his mom. As we were talking, Za walked out on the patio. "Hello, happy couple. Are y'all OK out here? Anything I can get you?" I could see she was lusting after Digital the whole time. "Digital, your little girl is beautiful, just like her daddy." Digital quickly put his hand on my knee because he knew I was at my limit. I looked over to Isis and handed her a napkin as to pretend not to hear what Za was saying. "Za, we are good and thank you for asking. We will be back in soon."

She walked away shaking that ass with force. "Digital, you better make up something really fast and get me out of here. I'm not one for ever embarrassing you in public, but she is about to push me over the edge."

'We just got here, that is how she is. I told you that already. You need to calm down and control yourself. I don't have time for drama."

"You act as if it is my fault. I'm trying to be nice and mingle."

"Well, you see how it feels to be hurt and jealous." As the words came out his mouth, I was hurt and embarrassed. I had hurt him so badly in the past and we decided to work it out. He has never thrown it back in my face before. I could not look at him because I did not want him to see the pain on my face or the tears in my eyes. He grabbed his plate and rose from the table. "Get yourself together and come back in. I will let you know when I'm ready to go."

I looked over at Isis and smiled and said, "I'll be in soon."

Fifteen past and I was ready to rejoin the party. I once again pushed all my anger and pain to the bottom on my stomach, so that I could make sure my focus was correct. When I walked back in the house, I noticed there were more little girls running around than before. Cody walked up and asked them if they wanted to play in the guest room. Isis looked at me and I told her to go play. As she ran off I noticed Za and Melanie sitting next to an older Hispanic woman.

"Chani, this is Cody's mom Alicia."

"Very nice to meet you, do you like your son's house?"

"It's very lovely, very lovely." I could tell that her English was very limited, so I did not ask any additional questions. Melanie looked at me and said the boys have come out of hiding to eat.

"Your son is so tall and he looks just like you. He's very handsome. Levi and I have three boys and they are so active. Right now they are playing football with the school. Does your son play any sports?"

"Not right now, he is waiting on basketball season. Za, do you have any kids?" She chuckled and said, "And ruins this great body, not happening. I can say that you and Melanie look great for women who have had kids. I heard that when you and Digital got married, you were already pregnant with your daughter. Is that why y'all got married?"

My voice was very flat; I did not know I was having a baby until a few weeks later. "Sure honey, we all have to do what is needed to secure our future."

"Za what's your problem?" I'm so glad Melanie said something before I could jump in, 'cause it would not have been good.

"What do you mean, what's my problem? Digital is a fine man and she is just average. I'm sure she had to do what she could to get him."

I just got up and walked off. Otherwise, I would have gotten into it with her; I would have been going to jail because I had kicked her ass, if I hadn't walked away at that moment. Payback is a bitch. In the dining room there were a few chairs open and I saw Digital sitting in one next to another man. I looked at him and smiled. He motioned for me to come and sit next to him.

"Cody has a very nice home."

"Yeah, he did alright for himself. Don't forget to give him the card."

I'm glad he reminded me. With all the drama it would have come back home with me. I pulled the card out my purse and handed it to Digital. We sat there for what seems to be for a few hours chatting with each other and people around us. I was so ready to go when Za walked into the dining room where we were. I sat up in my chair to see where Cody was and he was back on the sofa sitting next to his mom. I looked back over at Za and notice her hugged up with another guy. It seem friendly and I started to turn away when I saw her hand slowly caresses the small of his back all the way down to the bottom of his butt. As soon as it happened, she was moving away from the crime scene going back towards the kitchen. I leaned over to Digital, "please tell me you just saw that."

"Mind your business. That was all the *yes* I needed. She better hope we don't meet and no one is around to save her ass, she is all mine. I did not say anything more about it."

"You ready to head out, I need to get some real food, this not doing it for me."

"Yes, I will get the kids. I walked past the kitchen and saw Za and the young man smiling at each other like fresh lovers. All Cody had to do was look over and he would see. She looked at me as I past and she rolled her eyes. I smiled and gave her the bird, turn and walked away with my bad ass. I heard a chuckle and saw that Melanie had seen the whole thing. I smiled and though, *that bitch just don't know*.

I guess all the drama does not have to be in the office after all.

Chapter 9

Chani's Story

As we drove home from the party, Digital had the music up again so I was glad we did not do much talking. I could not help but think about the past and how he threw it in my face. I really hurt him. I often wondered if he did anything to get me back and he was just keeping it to himself so that he could really hurt me when the time was right. I don't think that was the case and I also did not think I could ever cheat on my husband.

Digital and I had been married for three years at that time. Living in California was great, but very expensive. I was very career driven and was working hard to move up in the company. Within a year I had move up from supervisor to manager over my department. I thought I had everything under my control. The kids had babysitters and I took care of my man at night. I worked 10-plus hours a day and brought home a very nice paycheck. What I did not see was that yes the kids had someone to watch over them, but I was not spending any personal time with my children. Yeah, I took care of my husband at night, but we did not talk any other time. I went to the office and worked. I came home and worked. I cooked a speedy dinner and did more work. When he asked me to talk, I would ask for a few more minutes and forget he even asked for some one-on-one time with me. I even noticed while having sex I was not into it. I would think about what I had to do in the office. The final straw was when I would work on the weekends. The office was closed but I was always trying to find a way to stay ahead of the mountains of work I had to do. I did not take the kids out, did not go to church and did not hang with Digital. I remember the day he came into our home office looking like a crazy person.

"Do you still want me? Do you want this family, this marriage? I'm so sick and tired of you putting this job before us. It is always about the job and the people on the job and trying to kiss their ass so that you can look better."

"First of all, I don't see you complaining about the money I'm making. When I'm able to cover all the bills and you can just have your money to play with. You know if I were a man, it would not be an issue. Men can work hard and do what they need to do. For me, I have to be a wife, mother and have a job. Why can't you step up and help me out for once. You are so selfish."

"I'm far from selfish; I want this marriage to work. If I did not care, I would be out there with whomever. Is that why you act the way you act, are you with someone else."

That thought had never crossed my mind. I just wanted to have a career. I want my kids to look at me and say, my mom did that for herself and did not have to depend on anyone.

"No, I'm not with anyone else." We just stared at each other for a few minutes. Digital is still glaring at me like a madman. I was shaking but did not want to show fear. He just walked out and slammed the door behind him. I can't believe that he just did that. Men always think that when you are not focused on them that you are focused on someone else.

A few weeks had gone by and I was scheduled to take a trip to New York for a business convention. This was a weeklong trip so I was making sure the family was prepared to survive without me. Digital and I were only at 50 percent speaking level. We were nice to each other but that was about it. Neither one of us took the time to really know what was going on with the other. I really wanted to be excited about going on this trip, but now it was just an escape.

"Do you want me to take you to the airport? That way you will not have to worry about parking."

"No, I get in really late and I don't want you all to be out waiting on me, I will be fine." I did not look up at him; I just added the final items to my luggage and zipped it up. As I was walking to the front room I called out to the kids to give them hugs and kiss them before I departed.

"Momma will be back in a week. I want you to call me every day after school and let me know you are OK. Isis, before you go to bed, I want you to call me and read to me over the phone. Blake, make sure all your class work is done. No horse playing in school. I don't want to get any e-mails from your teachers."

"OK, we will be good."

Isis was on the borderline of crying, so I gave her a big hug and told her I would be back soon. Digital took my bag and walked out to the garage. The kids followed me out to the car to get their final hugs. Digital was propped up at the end of my car with his arms folded.

"I left all of my travel information on the bar, text me anytime. If I'm not in a meeting I will give you a call." He did not answer but just gave me a hug. "Be safe." With that he walked over to the kids and they watched me pull away.

I have never been to the Big Apple and it was a challenge for me. It is a much faster pace than California. Man, I miss Texas. Not too fast and not too slow. I was the only one from my office who went to this conference, but I was able to make friends very fast. A lady by the name of Barbara latched on to me in our first meeting since our schedules were pretty much the same. To be honest I'm not sure who was tied to whom. She was a Texan and a true Southerner. Her hair was salt and pepper and she wore it short. Her skin was so tan that it looked almost like rubber. She told me about her home and that on her land she owned a lake that her family was able to enjoy most of the year due to the great Texas weather. Her dark brown eyes were big and bright compared to her very thin lips.

"So why did you move to California? I know it was not for the food." I had to laugh at that comment; I really did miss that good Texas food. "I was not running with a great crowd at that time. My dad's job had already transferred him to California, and after my mom left I felt all alone and scared. I had a baby on the way and knew I needed to get out of the situation very fast."

I remember the day I felt like it all came crashing down on me. I had just returned home from visiting my mom and dad. My mom knew I was struggling financially. She had given me some money to help me out. She had also given me a camera while I was there. We had taken so many pictures. When I got to the airport, my son's father was their waiting on me. Andrea was a nice-looking guy. Very tall and skinny and his skin was so dark and smooth. He was a lineman for the local electric company. He was very strong and was about 10 years older than me. I just thought he was the greatest. I still remember his eyes. I would call them cat eyes. They were very big and wide and they were light grey.

"He was from Louisiana and had a great Cajun accent. Instead of taking me home, he took me to my grandmother's house. He said our house was dirty and he just did not have time to clean up. He would pick me up later. I did not think anything about it. Few hours went by and he returned to take me home. He did a great job of cleaning up and I just thought about my bag. I left it in the car while I was at my grandmother's house. Andrea took the bag from the car and brought it into the house for me. I remember his uncle being at the house at that time, but I can't remember his name. Andrea told us that he had to make a run and he would be back soon. As I was going through the bag I could not find the camera or the money. I searched three times over. I was frantic, shaking the bag, sorting through the clothes. I was afraid to call my mom because they had already had suspicions that Andrea was on drugs.

"The reality just hit me like a ton of bricks and I just hit my knees and begin to cry. The only thing I could do was to grab my Rosary and run out to our porch. I began to pray, cry and pray some more."

As I was telling my story my eyes begin to water up. At times you think you bury those feelings and emotions, but when I speak it out loud it is like a floodgate. I looked at Barbara and I could see that it was affecting her also.

"So I'm crying and praying and his uncle comes out on the porch."

"At times we need a big bright sign to let us know when it is time to walk away. Chani, he is gone. This is your time to walk away. Take what you can carry and go and never look back. If you stay here and confront him, I will not be able to help you if it does not go well."

"That was just so weird how at the time I was praying for an answer it did come to me in a big bright sign. Some folks think that God has to rain down fire before they know he is speaking to us. It is things like that, which we have to be open to. I was still crying, but

I mustarded up the courage to go back into the house and repack my bag. I stuffed it with what I could. A week before this had happened I had a baby shower. I took all of those items and just put what I could in the back of my car. When I got in the car and started it, I froze. I was scared and just did not know what to do. I was 19 years old, and in a few weeks about to have a baby. I asked for strength and backed out the driveway. To make a long story short, I was able to get out of that situation and the baby, well young man, is a teenager now. Andrea is in prison due to other bad decisions he made after I left." My story had really touch Barbara and for a few minutes she was speechless. "God is good, all of the time."

The next few days were great. After the meetings we would go out and sightseeing. We ate meals together and really bonded with each other and other people on the trip. At night I would talk to the kids and make sure that they were doing all of their schoolwork, going to bed on time and saying their prayers. Digital and I had very brief conversations. I just told him who I was with and some of the plans we had made, but with no real details. Unfortunately, Barbara had to leave a day early so I was left with idol hands. The conference was over and I did not want to venture off alone. I have to make sure I go off on my administrative staff for not scheduling my trip correctly. I had an entire day in New York alone. My darn flight did not leave until 9 p.m. that night. Around noon I decided to stop being so lazy and at least get out a little. It was a little chilly out so I made sure to dress in what I would describe as cute winter wear. Skinny jeans, black knee-high 6-inch heel boots, cute tan top with a very thick warm black coat.

I walked a few blocks and saw a vintage bookstore. It was so cute inside. Nice and warm with a vanilla aroma. It had beautiful hardwood floors and, of course, shelves and shelves of books. In the center of the room was a spiral iron staircase. An older white-haired woman came down as I entered the store.

"Hello, how are you today?"

"I'm wonderful; can you point me to your horror section?"

She guided me where I need to be and I filmed through the books looking for an author that I had history with. Stephen King is one of my favorites and I had heard a lot about his book "Bag of Bones." I found a hardcover copy and had it in my arms as I continued to walk through the section. As I was looking at the books I heard the door chime as another customer walked in. I look up for a brief second and noticed a gentleman from the conference. He was in a few of the same classes as Barbara and I. He was a short guy, but he looked great in jeans and his white shirt outlined his muscles. He had short jet-black hair and wore glasses. He was of Indian decent but he did not have a strong Indian accent. Our eyes meet as I looked up but I turn back to the books.

"Chani, hi I'm James."

"Hello, how are you?"

"I'm good; I guess you are stuck here like me."

"Yeah, I'm trying to find something to keep me busy. How did you know my name? There were so many people at the conference."

He smiled, "Your name is very unique and you are very beautiful." I put my head down acting like a shy girl on the playground.

"Thank you very much. What type of books are you looking for?" "I'm a science fiction type of guy. It's always nice to have something to read on the flight home. I have been walking around trying to find something to do. I know there is a great restaurant about a block from here, if you want to grab some lunch."

"That sounds very nice, but I really need to get back to my room. My husband will be calling soon."

"I did notice the ring and I don't mean to be disrespect. I just wanted to hang with someone who was at least a little familiar. If it makes you feel better, we can talk about work."

I smiled and said "OK."

I go to the counter and check out. James was still looking for a book to read. "I will wait for you outside."

I thank the lady and walked out the door. I tried to call Digital, but it went straight to his voicemail:

Hey babe, I'm about to grab lunch with a co-worker who is still stuck here with me. After that I may check out a few more sites before heading to the airport. I will see you tonight.

James walked out as I hung up the phone.

"I did not see anything that I wanted. The restaurant is a few blocks south."

We walked in silence. The closer we got to the restaurant the hungrier I got. The aroma of the food was so sweet and enticing. It was an Italian restaurant.

"The food smells so good."

"The first night I was here a group of us visited this restaurant. It was very good and I wanted to try it again before it was time for me to head back home."

We were seated right away. "So what office are you from?" I asked him.

"I'm from the Miami office. I'm a district manager and I'm taking all this great knowledge back to my team."

"I'm from Fresno. I'm quickly working my way up the food chain. Right now I manage a small team. It's been a very crazy experience."

"Yeah people can really make life challenging. So how long have you been married?" he asked.

"For just a few years, we have two kids, a boy and a girl. My husband also works for the company, but in a different department. What about yourself?"

"I am married, no kids. I travel a lot so it is tough on the marriage. I do pretty well so she really does not have to work. I want her to stay active and we even talk about starting a family, but she is not really ready for anything I guess."

"This is my first major trip, but it sucks a little. My husband thinks I put my career before the family."

"I love a woman who knows what she wants out of life. You are very beautiful, smart and independent. I think it should be more of a team effort than just one-sided."

I must have tensed up because he smiled and said, "I'm making you uncomfortable again. I'm sorry; my wife said I flirt too much. I appreciate women. I think your husband should appreciate you as well."

I cut him off and said "he does appreciate me." I totally understand what he is saying about me being focused on my career. I have to check some of the things I do and make sure I'm not hurting my family." There was silence for a little while and thank goodness our food came out.

"So what are your plans when you are done eating? When do you leave from home?" I asked.

I caught him in mid-chew so he had to smile to get the food down before he could answer my questions. "I think I will walk around a little more. See if there is anything else I can get into. I'm not leaving until the morning. And you?"

"I think I will just head back to the hotel and make sure I have everything together. My flight leaves tonight."

"That sucks; I wished we could hang for a little more. You are very interesting."

Again our eyes meet and I felt a heat rise that I have not had in a long time with Digital. I know this man is a flirt. I know this is what he does, but for that second, I didn't care.

"I smiled and said maybe next time."

We continued eating, talking and laughing. When the check came, he pushes my hand aside and paid the bill.

"No matter what the situation is, a man should always take care of women."

I grabbed my items and we walked out the door. We were still walking side by side, but I notice he was much closer to me this time. Thank goodness it is cold outside; I did not want to start to sweat.

"I will walk you safely back to the hotel."

When we got back to the hotel, he walked in with me. When we got to the elevators he looked at me, "I want to come up with you. I know we have separate lives outside of this, but this is our time now."

At the moment, I was only thinking about myself and what I wanted. I whispered "do you have any condoms?"

"No, please wait here, don't run off." He walked to the small store in the hotel while I waited by the elevators. One percent of me wanted to run away. The other wanted to be with this man. Why? Was it because I had a fight with my husband, or because my husband was an asshole? There is no reason for this, but that 99 percent was telling me *who cares?* He came back after a few minutes and grabbed my hand. We did not speak while in the elevator and he did not push the number to my floor. There was no way for him to know what room I was in. We were going to his room. As I walked into his room, I was blown away. Being a district manager has its perks. "This room is nice. It's three times bigger than mine." He took off his coat and smiled at the comment. With my heels on I was a little taller than he was.

"Please, take those shoes off; you are making me feel like a midget." I smiled and move to sit on the edge of the king-size bed.

"So you are telling me you have not been hooking up with ladies since you have been here. This room is enough to get in the panties."

"Right now, there is one woman I want."

I took off my boots and stood up. He moved close to me and unbuttons my coat. He reached inside the coat and slides it off my body.

"Tell me, what do you like? What are your fantasies? I want to please you."

"I like to be touched with the softest touch. I like a man who is not afraid to touch himself while I watch. I like a man who knows how to use his mouth and make me super wet. I like man who can stroke it right and hit the spots. Knows when to move fast and when to slow down." "I'm glad you know what you want. I can't get anything like this from my wife. She will not even let me make love to her with the lights on. Does your husband know what you like?" "My husband loves sex, but we have not just sat and talked about what I want."

"Take off your clothes and when they are off I want you to lie on your stomach."

As I took off my clothes he also started to undress. It is very hard to be sexy when you are taking off skinny jeans, but I think I did OK. I kept my focus on him, watching him slide off his shirt. He took off his t-shirt and then unbuttons his slacks. I can see how hard he was from the bulge under his unzipped pants. I could feel the heat rise within me as I took off my shirt. I had on red lace panties and a red bra to match. I took off the bra first and slowly took off my panties. I crawled on the bed and lay on my stomach as he asked. I started to shake and not sure if I was just nervous or if I was cold. I could feel the pressure of him on the bed. He came next to me and turned my face to look at him. He kisses my cheek and traces his tongue down to my mouth. At first I only open my mouth a sliver, but as his fingertips caressed my back and go down to my butt, I was into him instantly. We were kissing so deep and so wet; I could not help but have an orgasm just with his touch. I could feel my wetness running down. His hand made it down to where I was wet and he soaked his fingers in it. We finally broke our kissing and he smiled.

"I love how wet you are for me." I pushed up from the bed and sat up on my knees. He begins to play with my breast and kiss my nipples. I noticed he was completely nude and the size of his erection was impressive. He grabbed himself and begins to massage it, never stopping what he was doing to me. I slowly moved my hand down to my clit and played with myself. I was so hot I just wanted to jump on him and feel him in me. I did not want to rush. I moved towards him and grabbed the hardness of him. I had to taste it. I put what I could in my mouth. Simultaneously I massaged the part of his penis I could not get in my mouth and played with anything else I could touch. He moaned and I loved the fact that I was turning him on.

He pulled back and grabbed my breast and pleaded with me to put them around his penis. He motioned as if he was inside of me. He stopped and I could see the hunger in his eyes. He got up from the bed and stumbled over to his coat. He was grabbed the condoms. He came back to the bed and sat up on his knees grabbing my leg, pulling me towards him. He spread my legs apart and me licking and sucking my clit. He moved to my vagina and stuck his tongue inside of me. He was sucking and licking all my wetness and I was grabbing at anything I could, trying not to run away. It felt so good. He finally came up from air and moved to my stomach. He was kissing and licking my stomach and slowly making his way to my breast.

While he was kissing and suckling on one breast, his hand was on the other pinching and nibbling until it is as hard as his erection. I could not take it anymore and he had that same feeling. He thrust himself deep inside me and I could not help my moan. It was so pleasurable and I wanted more, I wanted him deeper. He did just that. Each stroke was more powerful than the last. My hands reaching out to grab his butt, squeezing it making him more excited and with that he came. After a few moments of trying to catch our breaths he moved to the side of me and just clasped in exhaustion. I looked at the clock and only 30 minutes had gone by. I wanted to cry.

"I'm going to my room to get washed up and ready."

"Wait, you don't have to rush off." I just smiled and said, "It was nice but I have to go."   "Can I reach out to you?"

"Please don't." With that I dressed as fast as I could and got out of there. My room was three floors down and seemed like it took me forever just to get there. As soon as I got to my room I jumped in the shower and just cried. I cried like a baby. *Why did I do that? I had no reason to do anything that would hurt my family.*

"Hey babe, we are almost home, do you want anything to eat?" I had to blink a few times to get my focus back right. I had not thought about that day in a long time and thinking about it still brings me to tears.

"Whatever you get, I will just get something light."

"You OK, sorry if I seemed like a dick at the party. I know Za can be something else, but I did not want you in the middle of her drama."

"I'm cool; I think I'm just a little tired."

"Well because I was such a baby, I will let you tell me all about it when we get home. I know she likes to provoke people."

I did have to wonder to myself, how she knew so much about my personal business for a guy who does not like her very much. I will provoke that bear on another day. All I need tonight is peace with Digital.

Chapter 10

Ultimate Office Drama "The Christmas Party"

My office usually has an annual holiday lunch and afternoon Christmas concert. It is always very nice to see people in the office show-off their other talents. After the end of the celebration our company picks a child from the *Make a Wish Foundation* and grants their wish. That always brings me to tears. Digital's office, on the other hand, has a full-blown what happens at the party stays at the party event. Well, of course, we will talk about it and boy oh boy, they never disappoint. The company selected a very nice hotel to host the party. I like that idea because we can get a room at a discounted price and the kids can hang out in the room instead of being home alone. I love to be eye candy on my man's arm, so I always dress to impress. This year I selected a very tight, very black one-armed dress. It was cut at mid-thigh and hugged all my curves. The black onyx and rhinestone jewelry set really brought the outfit out. Of course, the 6-inch high heels and straight ponytail capped it off. Yes, this girl is bad!

As always, Digital was looking his best. He keeps it simple with slacks and a nice fitted shirt. He does not do the tie, but leaves a few buttons undone so he can show off a little chest. I don't mind the ladies looking at this power couple. *Looking* being the operative word. I was all done giving the kids instruction on how to contact us if they needed anything.

"Chani, you have the tickets?"

"Yes, they are in my purse."

"Sexy momma you look awesome. Give daddy some sugar." Isis giggled and Blake rolled his eyes.

"Mom, can y'all get a room?"

"We got one crazy. Y'all be good and keep those phones close. I will be checking up on y'all."

We made our way to the banquet hall. It was a beautiful setting. As you walk up there's a 10-foot Christmas tree next to a sitting area. This is the designated picture area. After we have our picture taken, we made it to the entrance of the party and I can say: this company really went all out. The stage was set up at the far back of the room. The DJ booth was to the right of the stage. Neatly decorated tables were placed throughout the room. They use a very nice cream-color tablecloth and large candles as centerpieces. Each table was covered in confetti and instant cameras to capture the moments. There was an open bar to the left as soon as you walked in the room and, of course, the dance floor in the center. Everyone was dressed to impress.

Levi and Melanie were inside holding a table for us. Melanie had a long red dress on with a long slit on the side. Embossed on the dress are decorative rhinestones. He red high heels matched perfectly and also showed off her legs. I walked up and gave her a hug.

"Momma, you look gorgeous!"

"Thank you so do you."

"Have we missed anything?"

"No, everyone is just filtering in."

As we are talking, the guys walk off to chat with other co-workers.

"There they go, leaving us behind."

"I love these parties, sitting at the table, looking at people I don't know and hopefully getting in a few dances."

Before Melanie could comment Za and Cody walked in. Cody looked very cute with his black and white suit on. What was really funny was Za's dress. It was a long dark purple dress with a long slit on the side. Embossed on the dress are decorative rhinestones. It's the same dress as Melanie's.

"Wow, do you see that Za is your twin." I thought it was funny, but the look on Melanie's face was pure hatred.

"That bitch asked me to help her find a dress. She wanted to look nice for the party. I did not think much of it because I need to find something as well. While at the mall, I found this dress. The funny thing about this is how bad she talked about this dress. Saying she thought it was too much for an office party. She picked out something totally different."

"She went back and got the same thing as you."

Cody and Za walked right by the table and she did not look my way.

"Where is Levi, I will need plenty of drinks tonight."

We got up and decided to walk around and just check out the scene. We found our husbands and they seemed very happy to see us.

"Chani this is our Vice President Dean. He flew in from New York."

"It's very nice to meet you," I said.

I could tell by his eyes that he had already had a few drinks.

"Digital, your wife is fucking beautiful." Digital and Levi laughed because they knew he was already wasted and we were not even in our first hour of the party.

"Thanks man, keep drinking."

"Hell yeah, I'm going home with someone tonight."

Digital took my hand and led me away. I took a quick glance and saw that Melanie and Levi were close behind. When we got back to our table we had some additional guests. Cody and Za had made themselves at home.

"So Za, I guess my dress was not too much for the party after all."

"What are you talking about; going shopping with you was a waste of time. Cody and I went back out the next day and decided on this dress."

"It is the same as my dress just horse of another color." Melanie had gotten just a little loud and Levi put his arm around her to calm her down.

"I don't know what your problem is, but we are here to enjoy this party."

"Keep fucking with me Za and see how much you enjoy it."

Za glance over at me and I had an evil smirk on my face. Before she could say anything more, an older lady was on stage was trying to get everyone's attention. The DJ stopped all the music and assisted her by asking everyone to take their seats.

"Who is this chick?"

"She is Diana, Dean's assistant," Levi explained.

Dean's wife must have picked her out because she was not easy on the eyes. She was about in her later 60s with a beer belly and curly fried blonde and grey hair. Her make-up made her look like a china doll.

"Good evening and welcome to our annual Christmas party. I'm so glad that we have such a large turnout. The more we grow it seems to get harder and harder to top the previous year. Before we get to the dancing and gambling, dinner will be served and we have some in- office talent that would like to show-off for you."

She looked over at her boss and knew he was not in any condition to make a speech. "Dean is making his rounds meeting everyone one on one. Leadership would just like to say thank you for a wonderful year. You all have come together and continue to work hard to make this company grow stronger."

As she was speaking, the servers were delivering dinner to each table. This year they selected grilled chicken with mashed potatoes and green beans, with a healthy salad on the side and sweet tea.

"Without each of you, this company would not be what it is today. The gambling tables will be open in about an hour. Remember the more money you win the better chance you can walk away with these prizes."

There were a total of 50 prizes that could be won. There were gift cards to various restaurants, bikes for kids, gift baskets and the big prize a $400 gift card to the Apple store. As I scanned the room, I saw the various casino tables set up and stationed in the corner of the room. How did I miss that?

"I want to be the first introduce the Sharp Sisters. They will do a few old-school songs for us."

As she exited the stage, three Amazon-looking ladies walked up on stage. The first song the DJ played was Soul Sister. They had their backs to us, but when they turned to do their act, I saw why they were so big. They were men dressed in drag.

The crowd loved it. I must admit, they did a great job. Each dancer was at least 6 feet, 5 inches tall. They wore different-colored silk shirts with skin-tight black jeans. The high heels, blonde wigs and great make-up jobs rounded off their act. As they were dancing, they walked off stage and took their act to the dance floor. Our table was one of the ones closest to the dance floor and they had their eyes set on Digital. I have never seen him so red, but when they pulled him out of his chair to dance, he was a great sport. The crowd roared with laughter and that egged him on. Digital did his best to keep up with the dancers, but laughter got the best of him and he had to sit down. As he sits back down we all held up our cameras to let him know that we were able to get some great shots, which will go on the internet as soon as we get a computer in hand.

The Sharp Sisters continued with a few songs from Diana Ross and Tina Turner while we finished our dinner. The ladies sat in silence as the men talked about the guests at the party. By the time the Sharp Sisters had completed their act, we were pretty much finished with our dinners. The singers were taking pictures with excited guests as the DJ began to play line-dance music for everyone to enjoy. Melanie and I ran to the floor to catch a few songs, purposely leaving Za at the table. I have not had fun like this is awhile. Before the party I practiced all the songs to make sure I did not look like a crazy person on the dance floor. After a few songs, someone was a little too close to my backside, and I made a quick move to get out the way before I notice it was Digital. He is a great dancer. The line dance was going off well and the DJ played a slow song for us to get close.

"I see you are enjoying yourself. Melanie seems like a cool person to hang with, we should do some family stuff together."

"Yes, I think that would be fun. We always talk about hanging with other couples and doing more things in the city. You have to promise me that if you decide to invite Za and Cody that you give me time to prepare. Something is truly wrong with that girl."

"I know she is a mess. I try to tell Cody how two-faced she is, but he is blinded by that hot monkey."

I laughed out loud. "Boy, you are so stupid."

"Well, it is the truth. For a man to move to another state, buy a house and move a chick in only after a few months, yeah she is putting it down really well."

"You see that stunt she pulled with Melanie and the dress."

"Yeah, what happened with that?"

"Za asked Melanie to take her shopping for the party. I guess she wanted to get a sense of how to dress. Melanie picked out the dress she has on and Za criticized her for buying it. Now look, she went out and got the same dress. I think if y'all were not here, they would have been fighting."

"Wow! That is why I do my best to stay away from that girl." When he said that I thought back to the housewarming party and how she attacked me with personal details of my life.

"You know, for someone who stays away from her, she sure knows a lot about our business."

He did not miss a step in our dance or was fazed about my smart comment. I didn't want it to come out that way, but oh well.

"Well, when she was first hired, I tried to be cool with her. I'm cool with everyone. When I saw how she was, I backed off. That girl was after me like a cop at a donut convention. I thought I told you about that."

"Nope, I would have remembered."

"Oh well, she just wants to be the center of attention."

I pulled closer to him not wanting to push the issue any further. He was getting his buzz on and having a great time. I knew he was not giving me all the details because one thing I know about Digital is that he does not tell too many folks our business, especially a bitch.

An hour had gone by and we were all having a great time. Drinking, dancing and meeting new people. We were all sitting at the table when Levi told Digital to focus his attention at the door. We all had to look. There were two men just walking in. They were very nice-looking guys. You could tell that they worked out or did their best to look their best. One gentleman had dark hair and dark eyes. He had on a white suit with a black vest. He had a cigar in his mouth, but it was not lit. To make him look fancy he had a white scarf around his neck with black tassels at each end.

"That's Carlos; he works with us in the office. You would never know it but he is almost 60 years old. We call him *pretty boy* Carlos. He's always looking in the mirror."

"Wow, he does look great for his age." The name went with him well.

"Who is the other guy with him," Za asked.

"I'm not sure; I guess that is one of his homeboys." Digital sat back in his seat and said, "Yeah, Carlos is a pimp. He is always in Vegas or just traveling with bad chicks. He knows how to have a good time. Levi you've been out with him right?"

"Digital, Carlos and I went to Vegas and man I came back so broke fooling with him. He likes to go all out, but I'm with you. I'm not sure who the dude is that is with him."

I watched as Carlos made his way from table to table speaking to every guest who was already enjoying that party. The other young man who entered the party with him was seated at a table in the back.

"Digital, Levi, Cody my man what's going on amigo?" Carlos has a strong Cuban accent. Now that was sexy. The men stood up to great each other.

"Carlos this is my wife Chani, Levi's wife Melanie and you know Za." He walked over and kissed my hand "now you are beautiful. Digital, you need to show off your wife more man. And Melanie, you are very, very sexy."

He walked right past Za. "Carlos, you are not going to speak to me."

"Sure, fuck you."

"Man Carlos, chill out and stop disrespecting my woman. You will make her upset."

"I don't give a fuck about her. She tried to play me for a fool and I tried to warn you about her, now you have gone and knocked her up."

We all just looked in horror. OK, if Cody wants to date a scank, that is his business but I guess we were all hoping he would see how she really was before they got too serious. I guess that plan just flew out the window. Cody looked confused.

"What do you mean knocked up? Za are you having a baby and did not tell me."

Oh lawd, this is getting good. "How the fuck does Carlos knows and I don't. Hell, how did you get pregnant by me, you only let me touch you one time."

I was done. This bitch is truly crazy. "Cody sweetie, I'm not having a baby. I just said that so he would stop being so mean to me."

"How in the hell does that make any sense." At that point I notice Cody's face and how red and angry he was. I also notice that he did not stutter one time while going off on Za. She did not blink, did not show any emotions.

"Well, I tell you what, we can finish this conversation later, and I'm out."

She got up from her seat and stormed out the room. Cody sat down and looked defeated. Digital walked over to him.

"Man are you OK, do you want to take a walk? Get you some fresh air?"

Cody did not say anything, but she got out of his seat and all the men walked out the room. Melanie looked at me and we both started to laugh at the same time. It was a good thing the music was playing so loud in the room. No one even noticed the commotion at our table. "Man, I wished I would have gotten to her first. I wanted to kick her ass so bad for coming in here with my dress on."

I continued to laugh and sat back in my chair. I notice the party planners passing out fake money to each table.

"Looks like they are about to open the casino for business. Diana made her way back up on stage for a brief announcement.

"Excuse me ladies and gentlemen. As you can see, we are about ready to open our casino. On each table there should be a box of play money for you to get started with. The DJ will play a few more songs and then we will move the tables to the dance floor. Casino play will go on for three hours. After that we will start the auction for the prizes we displayed earlier. Thank you."

The DJ began to play more dance music. Melanie and I made our way back to the dance floor. As we were dancing, I noticed the guys making their way back minus Cody. I tapped Melanie on the shoulder.

"Check it out; Mr. Cody is not with the guys. I guess he went back to his room to have it out with Za."

All the guys made their way to the dance floor. Digital and I were dancing when I noticed Carlos dancing alone.

"Aww, why didn't Carlos bring a date?"

"Good questions, he seems never to have any issues finding one."

As we were dancing Digital noticed someone on the floor he wanted me to meet.

"Hey, come walk with me, I want you to meet Mr. Jake. I told him you are from Texas and he always asked who your people are. He thinks he knows everyone."

He grabbed me by the hand and guided me in the direction of Jake. Jake was and older guy, short, fat and stubby. He was dancing with a tall skinny woman. I chuckled at the site. Before we could reach him, I saw Carlos out of the corner of my eye. He was making his way to Jake as well and the look in his eye showed that it could not be good.

"Does Carlos always pick fights?"

Before Digital could answer, we saw what was really going on. Carlos began to dance with Jake. Jake did not have a clue who was up on his back side so he started to back it up. The lady who was with him was in shock and quickly exited the situation. When Jake turned and saw who it was, he was speechless. He did a quick look to see that yes people were still dancing, but yes, they were looking as well. As he tried to back away from Carlos, he ran into someone else who started to dance with him. It was the young man who Carlos had brought to the party.

"What the hell is this?"

"Digital, I think we should talk to Jake later, he has some issues to deal with." Digital repeated, "what the hell."

I reversed the hold he had on my hand and pulled him back to the table. Levi and Melanie were still on the floor dancing and I think they missed the whole encounter. Digital looked lost and shocked at the same time.

"I don't get it, that dude is always with bad chicks."

"Maybe he is just drunk and playing games."

"Man, I just don't get it." At that moment, they started to clear the dance floor. Levi and Melanie came and sat back down at the table.

"Man, did you see Jake and Carlos?"

"No, what happened?" "

I will tell you about it later, I have to get my mind right."

I jumped in quickly to change the subject. "So is Cody OK?"

"No, we will check on him later, he wanted to go to the room and check on Za." As he was saying that I thought about the kids.

"Digital, I will go and check on the kids before I get into the casino games."

"Do you need me to walk with you?"

"No, I will be OK, it will not take long."

As I walked out the doors, I looked back at the table and saw that Levi and Digital had started talking. I wonder if he was telling him about Jake. I will have to ask him later how he reacted and what his theory was. I looked at the corner table and saw Carlos and his friend watching the room. I smiled and made my way to the elevators. The hotel was crowded and it took longer than expected for the elevators to settle on the first floor. Once I was on, getting to my room was not an issue. When I entered the room, I saw that Isis was sleeping and Blake was still up watching TV.

"How is it going?"

"We cool, I'm about to go to bed. Mom, can we go to the pool in the morning?"

"Yes, it is an indoor pool, so there won't be any issues. Well, it also depends if your dad is rushing out of here or not. I will ask him when I go back down. I was just checking on y'all."

"OK, good night."

I turned on a small lamp as he turned off the TV. I did not want it to be too dark when we came back. I whispered "text me if you need anything."

"OK."

I stepped into the bathroom to freshen up and then I left for the party again. Going down, it did not take as long as before. When the door opened, there was one gentleman on the elevator, but he had his head down and was on the phone. The first floor was already pushed so I just enjoyed the ride. "Hello beautiful, hello Chani." My heart started to beat really fast and my stomach felt like an empty pit. I was instantly nervous with heat rising up my neck. I thought I was going to pass out.

"James!"

For more Drama check out CJ's Website @

www.cjvaughnbooks.com

Like me on Facebook and Twitter